THE

HARDEST PART

OF THE WAIT

IS THE WEIGHT

*Don't Settle
for Less.
Wait for
God's Best.*

by

Barbara Dempson

she-attitudes
PUBLISHING

She-Attitudes Publishing
P.O. Box 124
Owings Mills, MD 21117
www.she-attitudes.com

THE HARDEST PART OF THE WAIT IS THE WEIGHT.
DON'T SETTLE FOR LESS. WAIT FOR GOD'S BEST.

FIRST EDITION

Printed in the United States of America

ISBN-10: 0996073205
ISBN-13: 978-0-9960732-0-2

Library of Congress Control Number: 2014905967

Contents

ACKNOWLEDGMENTS. vii

INTRODUCTION
Discovering My Truth 1

1 THE BLUEPRINT
The Road to Truth. 9

2 THE TRAP
Determination and Admiration 15

3 THE FALL
Shedding My Soul 21

4 THE CLIMAX AFTER THE CLIMAX
Discovering Truth 29

5 PLUCKING THE FLOWER BEFORE TIME
The Quest to Find Love 39

6 DEFLOWERING THE FLOWER
My First Experience 51

7 SEXUAL DETOX
Preparing for God's Best. .59

8 KNOW WHO YOUR OPPONENT IS
Playing to Win 65

9 NO MORE TEST DRIVING
No Longer Settling for Less. 73

10 HOMEMADE IS IN
The Decision to Wait on God 79

11 CREDIT WORTHINESS
*The Mistakes We Make When Choosing
a Mate* 87

12 NO WED. NO BED.
The Battle Along the Way. 95

13 THE WEIGHT
Waiting for God's Best 103

14 THE WAIT
Receiving God's Best .111

ADDITIONAL READINGS
All the Single Ladies. 123
All the Single Ladies, Part II: Recalculate 127
Choosing the Appropriate Level of Coverage. 131

ABOUT THE AUTHOR. 134

Dedicated to my daughters Jordan and Rachel

Acknowledgments

I thank God for giving me a chance to finish the work that I started many years ago. Back then, I set out to minister to and inspire women who had gone through adversity. But I didn't realize that I wasn't in any shape to minister to or inspire anyone because I too was broken, so I got distracted, and, as a result, it appeared my dream had died. Consequently, God reminded me that my dreams had not died, just been put on hold temporarily while he allowed me the time that I needed to make better choices in life. I thank God for remembering me. I thank God for a second chance to minister to and inspire a nation of women who are hurting as a result of poor relationship choices. And, I thank God for using me to help women discover their truth so that they can receive the very best from God.

I would like to acknowledge my four beautiful children, my sons, Torian and Jamel, and my daughters, Jordan and Rachel. Words could never describe the breadth of my love for you. You are my loves and you are my life. Each of you has given me a reason to live. In everything that I have accomplished, from writing this book to building a successful business, my greatest achievement is being your mom. You give me purpose and you give me joy. I'm grateful and thankful that God chose me to be your mom. Thank you for loving me in spite of the choices that I made, and thank you for your forgiveness.

I would also like to acknowledge all the people who support She-Attitudes™. Thanks for your love. Thanks for your support. Thanks for your friendship. Thanks for believing in She-Attitudes™ and thanks for sharing us with others. Thanks for giving us the opportunity to transform your life, restore your faith and help you rediscover your purpose so that you may reach your destiny.

INTRODUCTION

Discovering My Truth

"Sometimes we have to reveal a little of ourselves in order for others to be blessed."

BARBARA DEMPSON

hose of you who know me and are familiar with the work that I do through She-Attitudes, LLC are aware that I was once a victim of domestic violence. You are probably thinking that this book is about domestic violence. In this book, I do provide you with glimpses of that period in my life, and I support organizations that provide services to families confronted with domestic violence, but, surprisingly, this book is not about domestic violence. This book is about truth. Discovering our truth.

As diabolical as domestic violence is, I faced my greatest opponent after fleeing my marriage. In order to flee quickly from the abuse, I was forced to escape into the wilderness. The wilderness proved to be a safe place for me should the enemy come after me because I could hide behind a tree or cover myself with leaves to camouflage my hiding place.

The wilderness was a gloomy place, void of life. My time in the wilderness was dark and lonely. I spent most of my time collecting and reassembling the fragments of my life. I reflected on my past, reliving the hurt with every reflection. I was forced to rewind the tape and replay the scenes day after day. Frame by frame, I re-enacted each scene as each one represented a fragment of my life. As the pieces started to come together, I was then able to see my life in full view and examine its content. Upon closer inspection, seems the person who hurt me the most was me. I was my greatest opponent.

❋ ❋ ❋ ❋ ❋

The wilderness is where I discovered my truth.

The wilderness taught me three things: I learned a lot about myself, I learned a lot about people, and I learned that *everything* centers on hope. Whatever you hope will happen, will happen. Whatever you hope will be, will be. Whatever you hope to be, you will become.

In the wilderness I got to see my life played out on the big screen. I was able to see my life in a form that I had never seen it before—raw and uncut.

I was also able to see people, the characters in my life story, as they were—uncovered, naked, fully exposed. It is through these lessons that I learned which relationships to hold on to and which to sever. Severing ties has always proven to be one of life's toughest lessons, and it is not at all pleasing to the soul, but when God reveals a person to you, trust the revelation because only God knows what's truly in a person's heart concerning you.

I entered the wilderness battered and broken. I was able to see who I was in parallel to who I no longer wanted to be. I re-imagined my life as a victor and no longer a victim, but in order to re-emerge as victor, I first needed to take off the bandages. I then needed to reclaim the promises of God so I could rewrite the pages of my life and make a new start. As my time in the wilderness was finally coming to an end, I spent each moment reading the pages of my new life and rehearsing the lines from my new story to remind myself of the new life that God had given me. I am now able to repurpose the broken fragments for a greater work—writing this book.

I wrote this book because so many of us women are on a quest to find love—*true* love. And, often, during our quest, find ourselves in relationships full of sex, but void of love. We confuse sex with commitment and an orgasm with love. The road that I traveled that led to my time in the wilderness was because I, too, mistook sex for commitment and orgasm for love. Unfortunately, the sex was so great and so powerful that it nearly cost me my life. But my road didn't stop there, I continued to travel the road in search of my truth.

When men make love to us we feel whole. When they are inside of us, our heart is so full that it feels like it is going to explode. Then it is over, and he zips up and leaves. When he leaves, there is a hole in our heart where his penis used to be.

Men don't make love to our bodies; they make love to our hearts. Seems logical to think when you're having sex that the man is making love to your body because this is where you feel the sensation during the act, but long after the orgasm, the heart is still bleeding from the puncture wounds. With every thrust of his penis, your heart is punctured. Every time thereafter when he penetrates you, the hole in your heart gets larger and larger. When he is done, you are left with a gaping heart that can only be made whole with his penis inside of you. So you await his return. When he does not return, you're left with a wounded, bleeding heart. So you go in search of your truth. You are now on another quest to find love because you need someone who can fill the hole in your heart and stop the bleeding. Before you know it, you have journeyed from one failed relationship to the next, giving away everything and receiving nothing but a wounded heart in return.

My hope is that every woman who reads this book will find her herself on its pages and discover her truth, truth that will make her forever whole.

The
Hardest Part
of the Wait
is the Weight

Don't Settle
for Less.
Wait for
God's Best.

1

The BLUEPRINT
The Road to Truth

The summer of a year I would love to forget.

I awoke at 6am as I normally would during the workweek. The sun was shining, the birds were singing, yet there was dampness in my spirit and no song in my heart. My boyfriend, a guy that I really liked and who I thought liked me, had told me that he did not want to see me anymore. Boy, was I hurt. I really liked this guy. I mean, I reeaallyy liked this guy. I thought he and I were the ideal couple. I was a single mother and he was a single father. We were both raising boys who were quite close in age. He was smart, charming, ambitious and very attractive. He had the most beautiful eyes I had ever seen. His eyes were his greatest assets. Our boys got along extremely well and became attached to one another and I became attached to his son. As the boys were building a pretty strong relationship I thought he and I were building a strong relationship, too, but, boy, was I wrong! We dated for several months and saw each other every day. Sometimes he would pick my son up from school and I would pick his son up from school. We would plan our evenings together as if we were a family—family meals, activities for the boys and time for ourselves. Things seemed to be going great until the weekend before the breakup.

He told me that he had plans to go to the club with friends. I told him that my friends and I had also planned to go to the club. So, we decided to meet up at the club. I couldn't find a sitter so I was unable to go and I went to bed. The next day, I received a call from one of my girlfriends. She shared with me that she had gone to the club as planned and was wondering

11

what happened to me. I told her that I couldn't find a sitter. She told me that she saw my boyfriend at the club.

What she said next put a dent in my heart. She told me that he came on to her pretty strongly and acknowledged our relationship as nothing more than a friendship. Huh. Excuse me—nothing more than a friendship! I'm taking care of your son and taking care of you and we are just friends? My first reaction was to kill him, but first I needed to sweep up my fragmented heart as it had fallen out of my chest and shattered. I told her I appreciated her telling me and I would talk to her later. After hanging up, I immediately called him. He did not answer on my first *twenty* attempts. After calling him over a period of two days and leaving messages, I finally got a call back. Before I could say anything, he said he had decided that he did not want to see me anymore. I was hurt but angry. So you break up with me and give me no explanation, and I want to tell you how your actions affected me and I don't get the chance to. I was hurt, angry, shocked and somewhat in disbelief. How could this happen? Why did this happen? Did I miss something? Was I not paying attention? So many questions went through my mind with no answers.

Although the reason wasn't clear to me, he had a reason. Quite frankly, a man doesn't have to give you a reason why he doesn't want to see you anymore. I felt like I wanted to just lay down on a train track because being run over by a train couldn't possibly hurt as much as my heart was hurting.

After getting out of bed on this beautiful sunny morning, I began my normal routine, which included turning on the radio, then making my way into the bathroom. My heart was heavy. I stared at my reflection in the bathroom mirror asking myself, "Why?" Why me?" The hardest part was how to deal with the questions coming from my son regarding the breakup. This taught me not to introduce my children to anyone I was dating unless we were serious and committed.

Weeks later, this same girlfriend, who had shared this information with me and was now feeling sorry for me, called and told me that she had a guy in mind who she thought would be perfect for me. Of course I asked all the questions anyone would ask regarding a blind date. First, is he good looking? Second, does he have all of his teeth? Third, fourth and fifth – does he work, have his own car and live on his own, or does he live with his mama? According to her, he passed the test. I told her to give him my office number and have him call me so we could set up a time to meet.

Instantly, I am excited about life once again and thinking that maybe this guy is the one. I quickly got dressed and for the first time in weeks I am looking forward to going to work. As fate would have it, shortly after arriving to the office, my phone rings. Could this be him? I was a bundle of nerves.

As my phone rang, I just sat there like an idiot watching it. Finally, I decided to pick up. Sure enough, it was Him! We chatted for a few minutes and I invited him over to my place after work to become more acquainted. A mistake that I later learned—don't ever invite anyone to your house on the first date, especially someone you don't know, but, hey, this was more than twenty years ago and I didn't know any better. He arrived at my place promptly at 7pm as we had arranged. He was well dressed, and he smelled wonderful. I invited him in. He wasn't big on conversation and was rather boring. He also was not everything my girlfriend said he would be. He was not tall and he was not my type. However, he did work, have his own house, his own sports car and was ambitious. He was a man with a plan. None of this impressed me because I was 20-something years old at the time, and as with most 20-year-old women, the physical is the only thing that counts. The man of my dreams would have to be fine and I was not about to settle for anything less. At this tender, *unsaved* period in my life, my ideal man could best be described as tall (6'1" to 6'6"), dark—milk chocolate like Gerald Levert, beautiful white teeth like Gerald Levert, sexy like Gerald Levert, razor stubble beard like Gerald Levert, big, husky and strong like Gerald Levert, pretty lips like Gerald Levert. Yep. You guessed it. I was once and still am Gerald Levert's No. 1 fan.

After entertaining my blind date for about an hour, I took a call from my girlfriend inquiring how the date was going. I gave her the details in code. Once I shared the details or lack thereof, she asked if I wanted to go to the club. It was a Thursday night and I did not feel up to going. Besides, she had set me up on a blind date that was not going well. In as much as I did not want to go to the club, this would provide me the perfect excuse to get rid of this guy. I lied and told him that I enjoyed his company and that I would be in touch, but unfortunately had to cut the evening short because of a prior commitment. He was a real gentleman. He kissed me on the cheek and left quietly. Thank God, I did not have to fight him off or call the police to escort him out. Not all of my dates ended so peaceably. As you can see, I was batting zero in the field of dating. I was striking out all over the place.

By most standards, I was a pretty girl, sexy, great hair, smooth skin, nice teeth, smart, and I could hold a pretty interesting and intelligent conversation. With as much as I thought I had going for me, surely, I could find a replica of Gerald Levert.

2

THE TRAP
Determination and Admiration

We left for the club around 9:15pm. I invited my cousin to tag along, so she came to my apartment to pick me up. The plan was for us to meet my girlfriend at the club. I thought to myself, "This is my night." No question, I was going to meet Mr. Right. I had confessed out of my mouth everything I wanted in a man and I was determined not to be by myself. I desired to have a man in my life and on this night there would be no striking out.

As we were approaching the entrance to the club, there *he* was, leaning on a car outside of the club with two other guys. As we walked past, he smiled and said "Hello." His smile lit up the night sky. His teeth were *perfect*. I said, "Hello," smiled at him and made my way into the club.

Shortly after going inside the club, I saw this figure with a bald head and pointy ears coming at me. Teeth looked like pearls, they were glistening. Out of the shadows he appeared. It was the car leaner with the big beautiful smile. He was fair-skinned, tall and lean—unlike Gerald Levert. He had the *perfect* body. He had the *perfect* approach. He was smooth on his feet and even smoother with his words. And, he had the *perfect* pick up line although I can't remember what it was because so many years have passed. Ooohhh, and did I mention that he smelled oh so good? His hands were *perfectly* manicured. Not to mention he was *perfectly* and impeccably dressed, and his shoes were not turned over. I thought I had died and gone to heaven. He was PERFECT! And to think that after all this time, I thought there was no one more perfect than Gerald Levert.

He offered to buy me a drink. I told him I did not drink and he said "good, because I don't drink either." He asked if I would like to sit down and chat. I was mesmerized the entire time we chatted by his good looks and pearly white teeth.

Moments later we danced and he was a great dancer— just my speed. I didn't like to dance with guys who carried on as if we were making out on the dance floor. This dude was a *perfect* gentleman on the dance floor. He kept a good distance. The DJ decided to slow things down, by playing *"Play Another Slow Jam"* by Midnight Starr. Let me tell you, this brother sang to me and he sounded pretty good. He held me close. I was so stiff. He took my arms and wrapped them around his waist. His body was soft. I allowed my arms to rest along side of me for fear that I would touch something I should not be touching. He remained a gentleman, even while we were slow dancing. He never allowed his hands to explore. He gently stroked my back and sang softly in my ear.

The night was coming to an end, and after spending most of it in each other's company, we exchanged phone numbers. He mentioned he was going home to Virginia the following morning and would call me when he returned on Sunday evening. I was looking forward to hearing from him.

The next day, my girlfriend called and asked if I had heard from him. I shared with her details of the things he and I had discussed at the club the night before. She said she did not feel comfortable regarding him and in her opinion, he looked like the devil. I thought—this is nonsense. I gave her 101 reasons why I knew he was the one for me.

I expressed to her, as I reminded myself, how attractive he was. His approach was different, unlike any of the other guys who had come on to me. He appeared knowledgeable and well versed in every topic we discussed. He had the perfect body, the perfect teeth and the brother smelled good. He was also a pretty good singer. In everything he did and from everything I could see he was absolute *perfection*!

Sunday arrived and I had been anxiously awaiting his call all day. I had given him my home phone number, my work phone number and my cell phone number to ensure that I would not miss his call. Talk about overkill! Finally, he called my home around 6pm. We spoke for approximately an hour. The conversation was one of the best I'd had in a long time. He spoke well, used proper pronunciation of words, and used the proper tense and subject-verb agreement. He spoke like a scholar. His words were like butter. They flowed so smoothly. He wasn't loud or obnoxious as some of my dates had been. He spoke with a calm soft voice.

I shared with him some of my experiences, my hurts and pains and that I had decided I wanted to live for Christ. He shared with me that he was saved and that he supports me in my walk with Christ. He told me that we should both stop going to the club and listening to secular music. I shared with this guy that I did not want to hurt anymore but wanted to find peace and true love in my life. After pleasurable conversation, I invited him over.

We lived in neighboring cities, a 30-minute drive apart. He arrived around 8:30pm. His cologne filled the air and I hadn't even opened the door yet. I could smell his cologne as it filtered under the door. My heart was palpitating. I opened the door and there he stood in the doorway, with his teeth glistening. He wore a pair of jeans that were fitting like a glove. This man had the finest set of buns I had ever seen on a man. He also wore a low-cut vest with no shirt underneath, and he had an athletic build, lean and tight. The combination of his cologne, his pearly white teeth and his body were making my kitty holler, but somehow I managed to keep my cool.

After snapping back to reality, I invited him in. The date was getting off to a good start. We watched television, then listened to music and exchanged pleasantries as the hours flew by. There were two things that I pondered in my mind as we shared the evening. One, was he a good kisser and two, was he a good lover? I couldn't help but allow these thoughts to overtake my mind because everything else about him seemingly was so *perfect*. Surely, a good-looking man like him was a great lover. I thought this would be such a waste if this package wasn't all together.

At last, the night was coming to an end and we had come to the part of the evening that I was looking forward to—the kiss. It was awesome. His lips were soft and his breath smelled like baby's breath. After the kiss, we decided to end the evening. As he prepared to leave, he stated that I would be seeing a lot of him. I walked him to the door and he kissed my hand and stroked my face and left to go on his way. This guy was alright with me.

3

THE FALL
Shedding My Soul

As the months passed, we became closer and closer, soaking up every minute of each other's time. He would invite me to his apartment every evening after work and cook dinner for me. He was an excellent cook. He would always set the table with a single rose and a bottle of wine, with jazz or gospel music playing softly in the background. His apartment was adorned with Christian paraphernalia—bibles, pamphlets, literature, cards, crosses, bookmarks, stick pins, etc. You name it, he had it.

He would spend time with my son, who was 6 years old at the time, and take him to football games, basketball games, etc. My son really enjoyed this time and took a strong liking to him. In my opinion, this guy could do everything, except walk on water. He even showed me pictures where he had portrayed Jesus in a play at his church.

Even though I had been in church all of my life, I was just your average pew warmer. I knew what I called the basic fundamentals of Christianity. Thou shall not fornicate, thou shall not kill and thou shall not commit adultery, etc. However, even though I had not always listened to the pastor's messages and would often tiptoe out of the church prior to the sermon, I could always remember the pastor saying "Repent of your sins and God will forgive you and your slate will be washed clean!" At this time in my life, not having a full understanding of God's word, "repentance" was the best thing God could have invented, and because of my limited knowledge and unwillingness to plunge into the depths of God, I would stay in my mess and repent later if I even repented at all.

Months had passed, and we still had not been intimate. I knew he desired me just as much as I desired him. The day had finally come. Tonight was going to be the night. I felt it all day and could hear it in his voice when he called to invite me over to his place for dinner. When I arrived he was playing John Coltrane. When a man plays Coltrane, look out, ladies. He is on a mission to get some! His goal is to introduce his soldier to your kitty.

After dinner, he sang to me, we kissed and slow danced to the music. He left the living room momentarily and went into the bathroom and came out with a bottle of massage oil. He took off his shirt in front of me and asked me to rub the oil all over his back and chest. He lay down on the living room floor and I proceeded to rub the oil all over his back. He turned over and I proceeded to rub the oil onto his chest. This evening was getting pretty heated.

After I finished rubbing his body with oil, he grabbed my hand and escorted me into the bedroom. Brian McKnight was coming through the speakers. He had programmed a number of love songs to play in succession—one love song after another. Soon after that, the only sounds I could hear were the sounds of ecstasy. I had experienced my first climax. It was embarrassing but kept me wanting more.

The night suddenly turned into morning and we had not gotten any sleep. I realized we had spent the entire night making love. He was like a superhuman robot and I like an over-hungry lioness. It was finally time for me to go home and get ready for work. I left feeling like I had just shed my soul, but not caring at all because I was extremely satisfied and had reached sexual gratification, which I had only heard people speak of but never obtained.

While at work I found myself watching the hands of the clock, waiting for the day to end so that I could leave work and spend my evening with him. He called my office mid-morning to say "hello" and told me how much he enjoyed me last evening. He said he had been thinking about me during his drive to work and could not get me off of his mind. While speaking with him on the phone, the receptionist paged me and requested that I come to the reception desk. I hung up with him and walked to the front office. She handed me one dozen long-stemmed roses. He had sent them to mark our first intimate encounter or consummation of our relationship. The roses were so beautiful and the card was even more beautiful as he had written me a poem. I was so messed up that I couldn't work for the rest of the day. I just sat there anxiously waiting for the hands of the clock to strike 4pm so I could leave and return to his arms—or his bed.

Time was up! It was time to go home. I was so excited. I had not done any work all day. I ran home, packed my bags and headed to my man's house. He was ready and waiting to receive me. Every intimate encounter was more explosive than the first. My body would tingle, my limbs would go numb and I would experience shortness of breath. I felt like my soul had been sucked out of me. In fact, that is exactly what was happening. With every intimate encounter I could literally feel my soul being ripped from my body. It felt as if the very core of me was being distributed atop the sheets. Even still I had to have more.

✳ ✳ ✳ ✳ ✳

The days and weeks passed and every day the routine was the same—sex, sex and more sex. I had fallen in love. The devil had me. I just had to breathe the air that he breathed. If I couldn't, I did not feel like I was living. I knew that with him I was living because when he made love to me he would awaken everything inside of me. Little did I know that the devil was robbing me of my soul and planning to take my life. All the years of standing in the prayer line and having the pastor anoint my head with oil did not prepare me for the trap that lay ahead. The enemy was coming at me at full speed and I was enjoying every minute of it.

The enemy was not only robbing me of my soul but also weakening my spirit, rendering me powerless and in a total state of confusion. If the devil can rob us of our soul and conquer our spirit, then we would have no channel in which to hear the voice of God, and the devil can then lead us down a path of destruction—and down this path I traveled.

With every intimate encounter, the gratification became stronger and stronger, and my body became weaker and weaker. As I tried to pull back from him and revert to some sense of normalcy, like spending time with my friends and family, he would interfere with those plans and would make plans for him and me. I noticed he began to soak up every minute of my life. (Warning!) His plans would be fun, romantic and sometimes quite invigorating, but would always end up with sex. Each sexual encounter got better and better and the grati-fications were longer and stronger. We would go at it every day—two, three, sometimes four times a day. This demon was trying to destroy me, he had already dug my grave and I had absolutely no clue what was going on. In my opinion, this was the first time I had truly found someone who was everything I wanted in a man, or so I thought.

This sex demon was on me so bad that I could not concentrate on my job. My housework was slipping and I was neglecting my bills. My utilities were being shut off and I had also received an eviction notice. I did not care about anything except getting another dose of this man's poison.

There were times at work when I would be sitting at my desk and could hear his voice speaking to me, telling me to open my legs and let him in. I was slipping! I was hallucinating! The devil was playing tricks with my mind. I would look under my desk and there would be no one under my desk or anyone in my office. There were also times when I could literally feel him penetrate me and I would be alone in my office, my home or my car. I was in a trance most of the time. His spirit was so strong. It became part of me, and my daily living. The enemy had me fooled to think that what we had was normal and that we were in love. How could this not be of God? He is all I have ever dreamed of and everything I've confessed I wanted in a man. He had taken me to a level intimately that I did not think was obtainable.

These intimate encounters were not ordinary; they can be best described as addictive. I was like a junkie, an addict. With every intimate encounter, I expected a brand-new high, and he took me higher and higher every time. I'd scream and yell in ecstasy every time our bodies collided. After two years of courting, we had a son and decided to get married. During the marriage, he made me yell and scream even more, but this time it wasn't out of ecstasy, it was out of fear for my life. Turns out this *perfect* man, the man of my dreams, whom I had married, had my first climax with and was everything I wanted in a man, had a violent dark side.

4

THE CLIMAX
AFTER THE CLIMAX

Discovering Truth

*J*ust two weeks after we were married, he began to change. He became very controlling and began to lay down boundaries for me. I was not allowed to leave the house without him or without his permission. I would have to tell him where I was going all the time. I had to come straight home after work. I had to keep my cell phone on at all times. The abuse began with a slap. Then followed by a push or a shove, grabbing me by my hair or restraining me. It then escalated to punching, kicking, beatings with belts, clothes hangers and other objects and, lastly, death threats. As the abuse escalated so did the sex; the more intense the violence, the more intense the sex.

When a person is constantly coming for your body, you feel like you have something that is of value to them. So anytime he wanted it, I gave it to him. This was my contribution to the marriage. Back then, I felt as though I didn't have anything to offer but sex. I did not have to work. After marrying, we made the decision that I would stay home with our son. The decision not to work just seemed to make financial sense because I earned very little and the money that I earned only went toward day-care costs. My husband was an excellent provider and we never struggled financially. My husband had bought our house in preparation for our marriage, and I didn't want for anything when it came to material possessions. When the time came for me to return to work, the decision was my own. It was not something that he required me to do. My husband was an educated man and I did not have a college degree. He was handsome, smart and could have chosen anyone; certainly, someone more accomplished than me. So naturally having feelings of inferiority contributed to my staying.

There are other reasons why I stayed. I stayed because I believed I loved him and that he loved me, too. We had a child together and he had become father to my son. I had already experienced raising my oldest son alone and I did not want to find myself divorced and raising another son without his father. As this book is about discovering our truth, truth is, the main reason why I stayed was because of the sex. No matter how bad the beatings were, the sex always gave me a reason to stay. The sex was so great that it made me forget about the beatings. It was better than any bandage or pain medication. You may say that that is not an excuse to stay and you would be right. But let me say this to you… Never underestimate the power of sex; it's the reason that I have written this book. Sex is a healer for many. This is why we go from one relationship to the next or one sex partner to the next in search of it—in search of healing. Traditionally, people stay in unfulfilled relationships for two reasons: money and sex. However, there is a stark contrast between the two. Money may be extremely hard to come by at times, but we can always find sex. Whether you're a millionaire or a low-wage earner, you can always find someone to have sex with because sex is an activity that we can all participate in no matter the race, academic achievement or economic status. So, even if you don't have money or any way of obtaining it, there is always somebody willing to have sex with you.

Our first anniversary

We awakened as we would any other morning but this morning was supposed to be special. It was our first anni-

versary and our son's second birthday. We had planned
a birthday party for our son for that afternoon and later
we would have friends over for dinner to celebrate our
anniversary. So, naturally the kids would awake excited
about the day's activities. But everyone didn't wake to
the spirit of the day's festivities. My husband woke up
with violence in his heart. He was in a foul mood that
morning. A day that was supposed to be filled with joy
and love took a sinister turn.

I got the boys showered and dressed and allowed them
to play outside until my husband and I got dressed.
We had planned to go out for breakfast. He began his
morning with an argument because I did not invite
him to shower with me as we had done every morning
during our marriage. So, I invited him into the shower.
As we showered, he acted as if I was not even there. Not
one time did he even make mention that today was our
first anniversary and I didn't say a word.

After dressing, I gathered the boys to go out for breakfast. He could not decide if he was going to have breakfast with us. One minute he said he was going and then
the next he changed his mind. I told him that the kids
were ready to go and they were hungry and asked once
more if he had planned to go with us. He said, "No."
So I headed out of the house with the children and
headed for my car. As I placed the keys in the ignition to
crank the car, he ripped open the passenger door and
snatched the keys out of the ignition. He came from out
of nowhere! He pulled the door so hard it appeared to
be snatched off the hinges. It happened so fast; I didn't
even see him coming. As my children looked on in
horror, he pulled me from the driver's seat, across the
center console and the passenger seat, across our con-
crete driveway, up to our front door, where he pulled
me inside and threw me to the floor. I was thrown with
such force that I could not move because I had landed

on my shoulder and I was in intense pain. My shoulder felt like it was dislocated.

As I lay there in pain, he began to beat me. He kicked me about the back. He then picked me up off the floor. As I stood before him holding my shoulder, he punched me in the stomach and I fell to the floor again. As I lay on the floor, he kicked me, and kicked me and kicked me. My children were strapped into their car seats. I had no idea what was going on with them. The entire time that he was beating me all I could think about was getting my boys out of the car. I began to call on the name of Jesus. I may not have been saved but I knew enough to call on the name of Jesus. My grandmother taught me to call on the name of Jesus in perilous times. I had seen her call on Jesus and He showed up for her every time. I did not want to die. Not this way.

I continued to call on the name of Jesus. My husband told me that if I were to say Jesus again he would kill me, but I didn't stop calling on the name of Jesus. I had told myself that the devil may take my life, but my soul belongs to God. If I had to die, I was going to die calling on the name of Jesus. I began to call on Jesus louder and louder. My husband began to act crazier, as if the sound of the name of Jesus was piercing his ears. He was like a mad dog. He began shaking his head and walking around in a circle repeatedly reciting, "Stop saying that! If you say that again I will kill you!" Immediately, I noticed he was no longer kicking me. He was walking around like a crazy person, as if he was trying to figure out how he could get me to stop saying the name of Jesus. I kept on calling on Jesus. He then grabbed me and picked me up and threw me across the room. He jumped on top of me and muffled my mouth and told me to please stop saying that. Again, I would not stop calling on Jesus because I saw that it was working. I finally began to see that the name of Jesus was sending that demon aflight. Suddenly my body began to tingle. It started in my feet and was like a burning sensation. It began to work its way up, and as it traveled up through my body, I could no longer feel the pain of his blows. Before I knew it, I was back up on my feet standing face to face with him. I was still calling on the name of Jesus. I looked him in his face and said, "Jesus!" He said "I am going to kill you!" I said, "Jesus!" We went back and forth. I had become very confident at this point because I knew God was with me. I was certain that God would not let me die and that I would live. As I stood face to face with my husband, I looked into his eyes. His eyes were completely black. The entire eye was black, even the sclera. I knew I was face to face with a demon and this demon was determined to take me out. Mind you, the entire time this was going on, our children were sitting in a hot car in the middle of summer with the windows rolled up and this had been going on for approximately 20 minutes. I did not have the word of God in me because I had not read the word, so all I could do was call on the name of Jesus. Out of nowhere it was like a hand from heaven came down and pushed him over to the other side of the room. He was in the corner shivering and crying like he has seen a ghost. A mist filled the room and it looked as if there was a film, a haze or cloud of smoke in the room. I continued to call on the name of Jesus, and as he was starting to come out of the corner, the haze lifted and there was a peace in the room. He immediately ran to my side and asked me what he had done. I started in the direction of the door to get the boys out of the hot car and he grabbed my arm and cried like a baby. He then tried to make love to me as he had always done after every violent episode.

Whether I wanted to or not he would always seem to get his way. Sex seemed to be his "cool down." After beating my body he would immediately afterward sex my body.

After sex he turned back into the calm and peaceful man that I fell in love with and married.

Of all of the violent encounters and beatings that was by far the worst. Usually the extent of his abuse was slapping or shoving although at times he did beat me with his belt and once with a wire hanger. But this attack was more sinister. He beat me savagely. To this day, my injured shoulder has never completely healed.

Later that day, he began to open up and share with me things I had never known, things about his family. I discovered that his father physically abused his mother and his grandfather physically abused his grandmother, so this was normal for him. This is why it is so important to know who we are getting involved with. Often, we have no clue who we are dating. We don't know because we don't ask enough of the right questions. When I went through the abuse in my marriage, it was the late 1990s and nobody was talking relationships. Now there is relationship advice everywhere.

After enduring horrendous physical, mental and emotional abuse, I left my husband. You would think that things would get better. My world fell apart even more. When I left, I did not take anything that was of material worth. I was blessed to have my life and my children and that was all I wanted. I had not prepared myself financially and I was expecting another child. The financial burdens I endured were unbelievable. I filed for bankruptcy twice. I had no money to feed my children and could not afford to clothe them. I had to depend on friends and family for food and clothing for my children. A part of me wanted desperately to go back, especially for the financial relief. I began to think about the sex, our friends and our middle class lifestyle. In my mind I would play back how after every violent episode he'd apologize and say that he would not do it again, and how he would pacify my pain by making love to me and kissing my wounds. This seductive demonic spirit in him was so strong that when he would make love to me, I would forget that he had just beaten me black and blue. It was as if I was hypnotized. I was rendered powerless and enslaved to him.

My Deliverance

I did go back one last time a week after our separation. However, I did not move back into the marital home. The boys and I went for an overnight visit. After putting the boys to bed, he and I began to discuss the separation and the new baby that we were expecting. Later that evening, we became intimate. As I made love to him this time, I experienced something unusual. My expectation was that I would receive pure satisfaction as I had for so many years. But this time was different. This time I lay emotionless. There was no tingling of the body, no shortness of breath, no pleasure and no climax. How could this be? I was always his love slave. This was the one thing that I could not break free of and this would always make the pain go away. He didn't put his whole heart into the marriage, but he did put everything he had into bringing me sexual satisfaction.

This was the worst sexual encounter I had ever had with him. It appeared the blinders had finally come off. My eyes were finally open. I didn't even stay the night as I had planned. After the sex, I got up, kissed the boys and told my husband I would come and get the boys in the morning. I went to my apartment and cried before God. How could I be so stupid? How could I be so naïve? God began to show me myself. It was as if He was dissecting my entire life right before my eyes. He began to show me my husband and the wickedness that surrounded him. I cried uncontrollably for hours. One after the other, it was as if God was running it all off to me a hundred miles per hour. The visions were flowing, God was speaking and I was crying. From this night forward I never went back.

The Visitation

A few weeks after the separation, my husband's spirit would visit me. It would come to my bedroom at night and have sex with me. This demon had taken on a human form and would come into my room smelling of cologne, the same cologne my husband wore. It would start at the foot of my bed and kiss my legs and work its way up. It would press its body against mine. This demon was the same height and weight as my husband and when it rested atop of me it felt just like my husband's body. Its arms were strong like my husband's arms. Its legs would rest alongside me like my husband's legs. And when this demon penetrated me it felt just like my husband. It even made the same sex sounds as my husband. When this demon was done, I was completely satisfied. I was awakened by the climax of my body, but as I looked around the room there was no one there. But perspiration and body fluids remained, as if there had been an intimate encounter. I did not understand it at all until I spoke with a friend who was a minister and she told me that it was his spirit and it would continue to come unless I denounce it. These episodes happened quite frequently until I finally began to denounce them. Still in all, I didn't go back and we finally divorced.

5

PLUCKING THE FLOWER BEFORE TIME
The Quest to Find Love

After my divorce, I decided to start a women's support group ministry. I had named the ministry ENVISION. ENVISION is an acronym for Exchanging New Visions and Inspirational Stories in Overcoming Neglect. We would meet once a week at a friend's daycare center and begin our weekly meeting with someone leading the group in prayer. The ladies would share whatever was on their hearts—their hurts, pains, heartaches, etc. Some would share stories or give testimonies of how God had blessed them during the week. Every week we would share, laugh, shout, scream, cry and console. The ministry was going well.

Four months into the ministry, I met someone. I had attended a women's empowerment conference with my cousin. I was excited about going because my favorite band, Mint Condition, was performing. After the concert, as my cousin and I were walking toward the restroom, she was stopped by a gentleman with whom she exchanged pleasantries. She then introduced me to him. We both said hello and I walked away. She told me his name was Maurice and he was a friend of her husband.

Several weeks later, her husband called me and said that this same gentleman had asked about me and was interested in getting to know me, and would it be okay to give him my phone number. I said yes. Shortly after I hung up, Maurice called me and we began talking on the phone every day for hours on end. After about a month or so we decided to meet. The plan was for me to drive to the city where he lived to spend the weekend with him. I made a hotel reservation for the weekend because I thought this was best, considering I didn't know him very well. Plus, I had remained celibate during my separation from my husband and we were newly divorced so I hadn't had sex for quite some time. When I arrived, I checked into my hotel to freshen up while I awaited his call. Shortly after I got dressed, he called. He told me to cancel the room and not to waste money and that I could stay with him. I thought, well, he seems to be a nice enough guy so I did just that. I figured he wasn't a total stranger because he was a friend to my cousin's husband. They didn't have anything bad to say about him, so I figured what harm could it do. I canceled the room. He gave me directions to his house and stayed on the phone with me until I arrived at his doorstep. When I arrived he was outside waiting for me. He kissed me, took my bags and we headed inside. Turns out I didn't go missing and we had a wonderful weekend. It was the best time I had had in a long time.

Fast forward into the relationship, we would see each other nearly every weekend. We would talk during the week for hours at a time and talk every night before bed until we feel asleep.

Maurice knew that I had been celibate and he never brought up the subject of sex. During one of my many visits with him, after a wonderful lunch date, we were both tired and decided to lie down for a nap. As we lay in bed, we held one another and talked. We then began to kiss. The more we kissed the more my body heated up. In the 18 months since my separation and divorce I had gone without sex. So out of my mouth flies, "Will you make love to me?" He looked at me in complete confusion and said, "You don't have to do this; we don't have to make love." I said, "I want you to make love to me." He repeated, "Barbara, we don't have to do this. I am okay with things the way they are." I said, "I know, but I want you to make love to me." He assured me that he was okay with the relationship the way it was. I could tell he wasn't too comfortable with making love to me. It wasn't that he wasn't attracted to me because he *was* very much attracted to me and desired to have sex with me, but he wanted to make sure that things were well with me first as the divorce was just made final. Additionally, I had shared my story with him and in doing so told him that I wanted to minster to and inspire other women who may have experienced what I had experienced. He admitted that he wasn't an avid church goer but acknowledged that his late mother was an evangelist and he had seen a representation of holiness in his mother, and things about me reminded him of his mother. Because of this, he steadily tried to talk me down but my body was burning so badly that I just had to have it. I couldn't contain myself. I had remained celibate throughout my separation because I still considered myself to be someone's wife. Well, now I wasn't anyone's wife, so to me this meant that I was free to have sex with whomever I chose. I am burning with lust and this dude is still trying to talk me out of it. He said, "I'll tell you what, I know it's been a long time for you, so how about I just help you take the edge off?" He said he could do that without us having sex. I said okay. He proceeded to stroke my body with his hands unleashing pleasure points that I didn't know existed and this sent my body straight into orbit. The next thing I knew my body was exploding and I was climaxing. Afterwards I looked over at him and said, "How did you do that? What did you do to me?" He just smiled and said, "You're in the major leagues, darling." After this I got greedy. Though I was satisfied, I wanted to experience more of him and again asked him to make love to me, and this time he obliged. Wow! It was awesome! After making love to me he asked me if I was okay. I couldn't talk. I was just lying there trying to figure out what had happened.

At the start of our relationship I was still very much involved in the support group ministry until we started to have sex. It appeared that the more we had sex, the less important my ministry became. I was eating, sleeping and breathing him. I would get calls from the support group members asking if we were going to have a meeting and every week I made an excuse to cancel until finally everyone stopped coming and eventually the ministry folded. All seemed to be going well in my life and in my relationship until we started having sex.

Maurice was a lot older than me—nearly 15 years my senior. He was also a tall man as he stood six feet, six inches. After coming out of an abusive marriage, his stature alone made me feel safe and secure. He was a towering man with a strong voice but a very gentle lover. He handled me like air, like I was a whisper of a woman. He didn't yell, he didn't scream, he didn't belittle or degrade me. He always made me feel comfortable. He would often ask me, are you hot, are you cold, are you hungry, are you comfortable, are you this and are you that. The concern didn't just stop there. When we made love, he would always make sure I was comfortable and that I was pleased. Every time without fail before we made love he would always ask "Can I make love to you?" If I said yes we proceeded to make love. If I said no we would just lie in bed and talk and cuddle. During intercourse he would often ask me if I was okay. He'd ask if he was hurting me and he'd ask how it was. When he wanted to change positions, he wouldn't just contort me to his liking, he would guide me through everything he was doing. He wouldn't proceed unless he had gotten an okay from me. There were times he would even stop in the middle of intercourse if he thought that I was the least bit uncomfortable. He wouldn't orgasm or stop making love to me until he knew I was completely satisfied. This was a welcome change from my marriage, because, you see, my ex-husband was a banger. All he did was pounce my back out and he called it making love. Because he was my first real relationship, I thought that was how sex was supposed to be. No foreplay of any kind just a few kisses and the pouncing began. This ritual left my body tired and sore. Also, my ex-husband had a very high sex drive. He wanted it every night, before bed and every morning before work. He said he couldn't sleep without it and he couldn't function at work without it. If we ever missed the morning hook-up he would call me on my job and ask me to meet him at home during lunch for a quickie. So when I met Maurice, his whole approach to sex was different and it blew my mind. He introduced me to a whole new way of having sex. After being with him I discovered that what I had had with my ex-husband was sex but what I had with him was something altogether different. It was new, exciting, pleasurable, and I loved it. When he made love to me he made me feel that the only person's satisfaction that mattered was mine. He would make love to me until I was completely satisfied. He would keep his motor running until my motor roared.

Several months into our relationship, Maurice and I continued our routine of talking on the phone for hours during the week as we looked forward to the weekend and making love.

One night after making love he turned to me and said. "Hey, let me ask you something." I said sure. He said, "I thought you said you wanted to be a Minister?" I said I do. He said, "But how can you want to be a minister and have sex with me? I may not go to church any more now that I am grown, but I do know that there are things that you shouldn't do if you want to be a minister and pre-marital sex is one of them." He also began to question me about my celibacy. He said, "I thought you said you didn't want to have sex until you were re-married." I said, "Yes, that's the plan." He said, "Well, why didn't you stick with the plan?" He said, "You didn't have to sleep with me. I told you I was okay with things the way they were." He then began to question if I was ever really celibate at all and had lied to him. This was the start of the deterioration of our relationship.

I felt I needed this relationship with Maurice and there were countless reasons why. I needed this relationship because I needed to feel like a woman again. I needed to feel special; to feel validated. I needed to feel desirable again.

My marriage was hell. I married a man based purely on physical attraction and sex. He was controlling, possessive, obsessive, mean as hell, and just plain violent. He beat me for anything he could think of. Then after he'd beat me he'd force me to have sex with him. While we were having sex he would pounce my body and make me tell him how good he was. I would have to pretend that he was the most awesome piece of meat I had ever had. There is nothing more humiliating and degrading than to be beaten and then sexed by the man you love. So you see why I needed this relationship. I needed to feel protected after coming out of an abusive marriage and, most of all, I needed to feel loved.

I made several mistakes with Maurice. The biggest mistake I made was that I slept with him, something I never should have done. He didn't require this from me. He was completely okay with the way things were and even after I asked him to make love to me he constantly assured me that that wasn't important as he just enjoyed being with me. I allowed my drawers to catch fire and soon after my relationship caught fire and burned to the ground. All that was left were ashes.

I made my greatest mistake when I went to his house. I should have stayed with my original plan to stay at a hotel. Unless you want to sleep with a man, never go to his home, on a long-distance trip or visit him in a hotel room. Because all of these things say to a man that you are down for sex.

Men process everything we say. When we tell a man that we are saved, love God, are celibate and will not have sex until marriage, the first thing a man thinks is: either she is the real thing and the woman for me, or she is full of shit and I bet I can get that. Then the tests come. Men take us through their own little tests to see if we are who we say we are. So when you say you are celibate, just know that he will put you to the test.

It is vital that we show men that we are, in fact, who we say we are. This is important because men like to know who they are getting involved with and what they are getting involved in. When we say one thing and do the other, it is a direct violation of trust in their eyes. When we tell a man that we can remain celibate and then we turn around and sleep with them, the first thing they think is that we have no self-control. See, to a man it's not about him, it's about us. You have to think like a man. Your mind tells you that if he didn't keep pressuring you, you would not have given in. But his mind tells him that she told me she wouldn't give in but she did. Now how many other brothers did she tell this same thing to and they got THE PANTIES too? Then their mind automatically goes back and replays every conversation that they've had with us. They begin to doubt everything we've said. We then become liars in their minds and can't be trusted. Then, just like day-old bread, they toss us out.

I can remember a conversation I had with a male friend. I happened to run into him at a Walmart store when Maurice and I were dating. I shared with him my situation with Maurice and how things seemed to have been going well until I slept with him. My friend and I talked for about an hour in the middle of the beverage aisle. He told me two profound things that I will never forget. He said it should only take a man six months to determine if he wants to marry a woman. He also told me that if a woman tells a man that she is celibate and will not have sex with him until marriage that she must keep her word. He said that his wife was celibate during their courtship and he pressured her for months to have sex with him. Although he constantly pressured her, she still wouldn't give in as her mind was made up. She wanted to be married first. He admired her commitment as a woman who would keep herself for her husband. He told me that after making a decision to spend his life with her, he asked her to marry him and they got engaged. After they got engaged, he, being a man, continued to pressure her for sex. She, tired of listening to his whining, finally decided to give in to his demands and let him have the kitty. He said that after he made love to her, even though it was very good, it triggered an abnormal reaction in him. He shared that instead of running to her, he ran from her. I asked what he meant. He began to tell me about his life before meeting his wife and the numerous women he had slept with. He continued to maintain a sexual relationship with some of these women during the courtship with his wife. He said what drew him to his wife was that she was saved and she told him she was celibate. He was not saved at the time, but this woman appealed to him because he was getting sex, plenty of it, and he had met a woman who had more regard for her body.

He believed he had something special but he wanted to give it more time to be sure. He said months passed and they continued to date and she would not release her kitty to him. He figured by now he would have stroked her kitten a few times considering his track record with other women. He went on to say that one morning he awoke to a voice telling him that it was time. He said at first he didn't know what was happening because he had just stroked someone else's kitten the evening before. He said he asked the voice, "time for what?" He said continually he heard the voice telling him it was time. He said he finally realized that it was God telling him it was time for him to settle down. He then got out a piece of paper and wrote down all the reasons why he should or shouldn't marry his wife. When he was done, the reasons he should marry her outweighed the reasons why he shouldn't. He said the two things that were at the top of the list were her commitment to God and her commitment to him. After that was the fact that she remained celibate despite his constant nagging, pleading and pressuring. I thought, wow! He went on to say, "Barbara, if you tell a guy that you are celibate then stick to it" because, right after he and his wife got engaged, she finally decided to give in to him and his response was not what either of them expected. He said after they had sex she became just like all the other women whose kittens he had stroked. I asked him how so? He said, "Because she let me pluck her flower before time." He said, "She told me she would not sleep with me until after we were married, and I had learned to accept that and live with it. So, after she gave it to me it was like, 'game over!' " I told him I could not understand how this could have had an adverse effect. He said he didn't think it would either, but it did. He said after he made up his mind that this was the woman he was going to spend the rest of his life with, he cut off all the other women and committed himself to her. After they had sex, he immediately reverted back to his old ways of sleeping around. He had gotten so bad that he decided not to marry her. I was standing there looking at him in utter shock, wondering if I should kill him for her, but, hey, by this time, they had already been married for more than 10 years. After sharing his story with me, he told me never to be afraid to tell a man that I'm celibate as this is my honor and it is an honor to God. Believe it or not, he said, to most men this is very appealing.

Needless to say, this information came a little too late for Maurice and me, but not too late for me to make a decision to do it again and to do it right this time.

Maurice showed me what lovemaking was supposed to feel like. With him I witnessed the art and beauty of lovemaking and experienced passion I had never known. I also experienced just how gratifying and satisfying lovemaking could be. Even if he had had a long week and was completely exhausted, he still sacrificed to please me. He knew how to take care of me without physical penetration. He knew my erogenous zones. He knew just where to touch me to send my body soaring. He showed me how he could penetrate me without penetrating me. Plus, he always took his time. He never rushed. He prided himself on making sure I was completely satisfied. Mind you, he didn't stop there. He talked to me every step of the way from the time he said "can I make love to you" to "you down for more." He always wanted to make sure he had my full cooperation and participation. And he wanted to make sure I was okay with everything he did. Before he would switch positions, he would whisper things in my ear like, "I am going to put your legs on my shoulder, can I go a little deeper" or "can I lay you on your stomach" and he would end every request with "Are you okay with that?" He seduced me with words. I was so overwhelmed with passion that I could barely whisper a faint "yes." His man meat and his words blew my mind.

6

DEFLOWERING
THE FLOWER
My First Experience

The first time I had sex I was 19 years old. I was considered to be a late bloomer by my peers' standard because most, if not all, of my friends were already having sex. Some of them started in middle school. Heck, I knew people who were doing it in elementary school. Not me. I was always too afraid. Especially after hearing all the stories of how bad it hurt. Plus, I knew my mother would kill me.

The guy I lost my virginity to was six years my senior. He had seen me around and inquired of me through a mutual friend. I was a little nervous about dating him because he was older and he had a reputation for being a cat slayer, and here I was, this sexually inexperienced young woman. He knew I was a virgin and was unfazed by the fact. Our relationship started out slowly. I still lived at home with my mom and had a midnight curfew. I had no dating experience because up until then, I was not allowed to date. I didn't drive so he would always have to pick me up. He lavished me with expensive gifts—diamond jewelry, and expensive clothes, shoes and handbags. I guess this was his way of fattening me up for the slaughter.

After dating for about three months, we decided it was time to do it! It was time to make love. Boy, was I nervous. As I lay down on the bed with him lying next to me, we begin to kiss—a lot! As we lay kissing, he began to work my pants off. He would pull down one side and I would pull up the other side. We continued this pattern until I was sure that I was ready. I don't know which I feared more. Having sex with him, or my mama! Either way I was in for beat a down. Slowly I built up my nerve and finally felt like I was ready to do it.

Once I got past the having sex part I had to deal with the going home part. How could I go home and face my mother? Would she be able to tell I had just had sex? I was more afraid of her reaction than how painful the act would be.

I was so afraid that I started crying before he even touched me. He told me to relax. He promised he wouldn't hurt me. I lay there snotting and crying thinking, brother, you are the least of my concerns—my mama is going to kill me! Then she'll probably put me out and I won't have any place to live.

It seemed like it took forever for him to finally get my clothes off and get me to calm down. It was just as Betty Wright had described. I was nervous and trembling waiting for him to walk in. I was trying hard to relax but I just couldn't keep still. The more he kissed me and caressed my body the more relaxed I became. Finally, I calmed down.

As he lay between my legs he assured me he would take his time and wouldn't hurt me. All I can remember is the pressure and the blood. He could only get it about a third of the way in. It took a few attempts before he could gain full entry. The more we did it, the more relaxed I became. The thing I remember most about this experience was him showing me how a woman is supposed to move her body so that a man could get pleasure out of the act. He told me that there is no pleasure for a man if a woman just lies there. I thought, now how am I supposed to know that, it wasn't like I had had years of practice. He taught me how to move my hips, how to press my pelvis into his and how to work with the rhythm of a man's body. He showed me step-by-step how to become participatory during sex.

We dated for a few months before he decided he wanted to move on. This was a devastating blow. It left me confused and depressed. The days seemed dark and long. I felt sick and feverish all the time. Looking back, I didn't think I would ever recover from this. I felt betrayed. I couldn't eat or sleep. My weight dropped to nearly 85 pounds. I cried every day—day and night. He had stolen my innocence, my heart, my confidence, my sanity and my will to live. He had turned me out, plain and simple. That's where my pain with men started.

Fast forward some twenty years and several relationships later. I have learned so much about what happens to us when we have sex with men. When we have sex with men, they take a part of us with them when they leave. Imagine a sunflower, its petals being plucked one by one. Once its petals are plucked it doesn't look the same. It is still a sunflower but because one of its petals has been plucked it doesn't feel whole as it did when it had its full bloom. It felt confident and creative. The moment the first petal was plucked from the sunflower it caused the rest of the body to suffer because something was taken that wasn't properly given. The flower that once stood straight and bright now tilts. The same can be said for us. Men go into relationships with the thought of deflowering the flower and we go into it with the expectation of commitment. We take every barrier down, thus exposing ourselves to be destroyed. Every time we have sex with a man who is not the man that God has for us, they take a part of our confidence, self-worth, and our identity. They take our self-assurance and a portion of our tomorrow; our five-, ten-, fifteen-year plan and our future accomplishments. Because when you take one piece of us, the rest of us is affected. If a car is wrecked and then repaired, it doesn't drive 100%

like it used to, but only the driver knows this. It may look good with its new bodywork and new paint job, but the driver knows that something isn't quite right. The ride is a little off. We are just like the wrecked car—battered and broken. One wrong hit temporarily takes our strength. It weakens us and some of us feel like we are not able to succeed in the next relationship. Now we feel like we have to lower our standard. We feel insecure and incompetent and it affects our ability to reason, and for some of us it opens us up to thoughts of suicide. We feel like we don't want to live any more. The wrong man detours us from our purpose in life. Some of us are able to get back on the road and some of us are not, and some are in prisons and mental hospitals.

When a man's penis is inside of us we feel whole. We feel complete. But when he takes it out we are left with a hole in our heart. Where your heart was once whole, it is now punctured. This is what happens when we have sex with men and the relationship doesn't materialize as we had hoped. Meaning... the minute he took his penis out of your vagina, it left you with a big gaping hole in your heart. Before the penetration your heart was intact. Now there is a hole where his penis used to be. The moment a man penetrates us, life as we know it no longer exists. We instantly change. We have a hard time staying focused. He has now become the center of our world. Some women don't even want their children around. The children that they carried, birthed and nurtured who were once the object of their affection and the center of their joy are now seen as a threat to their relationship. That's because we become paranoid. Especially if it's good! Everybody is now a threat. You now have to know where he is and what he is doing every minute of the day and sometimes who he is doing it with. So you start calling him repeatedly. You start doing drive-bys. You ask others if they've seen him, has he mentioned you and did he ever say he cared for you.

If you find out he is doing it with someone other than you, you then have to know who she is and what she looks like. You didn't do any of these things prior to having sex with him.

You know what our problem is? We don't watch the movie. We stay awake for the commercials and fall asleep on the movie. When we do this, all we are seeing are the paid advertisements and not the characters in play. Men study us throughout the dating process. They know where to caress us. They know how to captivate us with words. They know the right words to arouse us, to make us like silly putty in their hands. This way they can get everything they want. They set the stage to remove a petal and deflower us. They rob us of the gift that we have been saving for our husbands. And they take our minds in the process. Then, when they leave us, we feel violated and empty inside.

The most important thing to remember is this: The man is the one doing the penetrating. He is the one penetrating your body, not you penetrating his body. For a man, penetration takes place outside the body. For us the penetration takes place inside the body. When men penetrate us, they penetrate our body, our mind, our soul and our very existence. They penetrate our body—then our heart, but for them, it is the complete opposite. We penetrate their heart—then their body. For them, penetration takes place in the heart first, then in the body. For us penetration takes place in the body and then the heart. When they penetrate us, for most of us, we are instantly gone! For him, once his heart has been penetrated, the physical penetration seals the deal. Sure, he may enjoy the sex, but that is all it is to him—just sex. We can sleep with a man over and over but if his heart is not penetrated he will not be moved. This is why a man can date us for years and never marry us and meet someone else and within six months marry her. She penetrated his heart where all you did was let him penetrate you. But, hey... freely you gave and freely he received!

7

SEXUAL DETOX
Preparing for God's Best

few years after breaking up, Maurice and I decided to meet for lunch. We had remained friends and often talked, although we were no longer in a relationship. Having lunch with him reminded me of the times we spent together. All I could see the entire time was visions of him and me making love. I was so completely overtaken by lust that being near him made me a nervous wreck. My body went ballistic. I couldn't even enjoy my lunch. My mind was trying to block out the images but my body was enjoying the movie. Embarrassingly, I began to recall how I would scream with pleasure and how he used to say, "Damn, this shit is so good." Fortunately for me, I was able to maintain my cool, at least above the waist, but below the waist my cat was hollering.

After lunch he walked me to my car and I drove home. I was so messed up I could barely drive. My mind was saying move on, he doesn't want you, he's an arrogant jackass and if he really loved you he would have married you. My cat was saying to hell with you, I want some of that. She was remembering him as the last person who made her feel good. Even though we didn't have sex back then, I felt like I had fornicated in my heart. I had all but screwed his brains out in my mind. My heart was very heavy and I felt like a failure. I wondered how I could admit I'm celibate and live a life of celibacy when just being around this guy was making my cat spit fire. He had tried often through the years to talk me into surrendering the cat but by the grace of God I always stood my ground—no commitment, no cat! My body had been going through this ritual for years but this time it affected me differently. This time I felt like I had fornicated before God. Like I had just committed a sin. I began to doubt my salvation. I began to feel like something was wrong with me. I couldn't understand why every time I was in this man's presence my body would react this way. I also began to think that I was abnormal, that there had to be something wrong with me.

So here he was again penetrating me without penetrating me. I didn't yield to the temptation, but I still felt like I had just fornicated. I wrestled with this in my head. How long will this continue to happen to me? Why does this keep happening to me and when will these feelings ever leave me?

Fast forward, through much prayer and faith, those feelings eventually left me. Sure I can remember sleeping with him but that is all I can remember. That's because I've gone through sexual detox.

What is sexual detox?

Sexual detox is the purification process through celibacy that brings us closer to God and prepares us mentally and sexually to receive our husbands—the men who God truly has for us—not the counterfeits. Sexual detox is so necessary because in order for us to be sexually satisfied in our marriages, we have to fully detox our past lovers. Our minds have to be detoxed of the things that they *used to say* to us and our bodies have to be detoxed of the things that they *used to do* to us. This is so that we will make no sexual comparison of them with our husbands.

Purification through celibacy is an important process in that it rids our bodies of the slush and gunk that has built up on our vaginal walls. Celibacy cleanses our body from the residue that our past lovers have left behind, prepares our bodies for our husbands, and clears our minds of any debris that the previous occupants have left behind so that the new tenant can take up residence there. Though we will never go back to being virgins, celibacy gives us back a spiritual hymen. It makes us virginal again, spiritually. You go back to being fresh as a flower, youthful and cleansed. Our bodies need to go through this deep cleansing so that when the husband enters he is entering into a clean, renovated dwelling.

After going through sexual detox, we can tell our past lovers 'no thank you' when they tell us that they want to have sex with us. The once noticeable sensation that erupted through your body upon hearing his voice no longer exists. Your mind remembers sleeping with him but your body has no recollection of the feeling. You begin to wean yourself from things that will provoke a sexual response. You go through your cell phone and erase the numbers of past lovers because you no longer have use for them. You'll find that you no longer have a desire to watch movies and TV shows with high thresholds for sex. You lose interest in hearing your friends' sexual escapades and fantasies. The dirty jokes that you once laughed at are no longer funny. During your physical detox you take the sex toys and throw them away. The gifts of lingerie are also candidates for the trash. You cancel your porno subscription and throw away the KY jelly. When those moments arise when your body starts craving a man, you fall down on your knees and you pray. While in prayer God reassures you that if you just wait a little while longer, the best is yet to come.

8

KNOW WHO
YOUR OPPONENT IS
Playing to Win

*P*rior to marrying my husband, we had sex nearly every day for years—several times a day. It wasn't until I married him that I was able to see who he really was. His keeping me in bed was his way of camouflaging his true identity. By the time I realized who he was, it was too late. We overdosed ourselves in sex. I couldn't get enough of him and he couldn't get enough of me. My body would crave him. I was like a junkie. Soon after we'd have sex, I wanted more. But I didn't realize the message this addictive sex was sending.

When we had sex I would scream and beg him to stop all the while grabbing him around his waist and pressing his body deeper into mine. He understood that even though I would scream and beg him to stop that that wasn't what I really wanted. He understood stop to mean "go" and the screams to mean "go deeper." I finally got the revelation. I began to witness an eerie pattern. When he'd beat me, I would scream then, too, and beg him to stop. When he was abusing me, his mind registered my screaming and pleading as enjoyment. I screamed and pleaded with him when we were having sex and I screamed and pleaded with him when he was beating me. His mind registered both as something that I wanted. I thought, how twisted. This can't be true. But, then, I realized that after every incident of abuse that he would immediately force me to have sex with him, and during sex he would pounce my body so hard and the more I screamed the more he pounced. Then, after sex was over, he was back to normal as if the abuse had never taken place.

My marriage and every relationship since my marriage have taught me one valuable lesson. Always know who your opponent is.

Play to Win

If you're going to play, then play to win. Before stepping into the ring, make sure you're prepared. Make sure that you've had a chance to study your opponent. If you don't, you're like a boxer stepping into the ring without any knowledge of his opponent. A boxer, who sometimes trains for a year before a fight, never goes into the ring without first studying his opponent. The most important thing that a boxer wants to know is his opponent's record: Who did he fight and how did he do? He will spend hours upon hours watching footage of his opponent's previous fights. He wants to know who his opponent really is, what his weaknesses are and what his strengths are. Which hand is the fastest and which hand carries the most powerful punch? If you don't take the time to study your opponent before stepping into the ring, then you don't stand a chance at winning. I married a man that I barely knew then shortly after my divorce fell in love with a man who had a fear of commitment. Had I just taken the time to get to know either of them, maybe I could have made better choices in the beginning. I allowed the needs of my flesh to control my thinking. I was led into relationships full of sex, all because I confused sex with commitment and orgasms with love.

It is critical that you know who you are stepping into the ring with. Make sure you know as much as possible about the opponent sitting in the opposite corner. Because if you don't, then you have already lost before you have had the chance to win. Some of us will suffer a few defeats before we learn what it takes to come up with a winning hand. My advice to you is—if you are going to play the game—play to win!

Are you familiar with the Kenny Roger's song "The Gambler"? I love this song because I find it to be very insightful. The song paints the story of two strangers on a train—one the narrator and the other a gambler. The narrator shares the story of his encounter with a gambler and how the gambler offers him some advice that changes his life.

The narrator says that it was a warm summer's evening and he was on a train bound for nowhere. While on the train, he meets up with a gambler. He says that they were both too tired to sleep so they took turns staring out of the window at the darkness until boredom overtook them and the gambler began to speak. The gambler tells the narrator that he has made a life out of reading people's faces and knowing what cards they are holding by the way they held their eyes. He also tells the narrator that he can tell that he (the narrator) is fresh out of aces.

What does the gambler mean when he tells the narrator that he is fresh out of aces? Aces represent power, so if you have no aces—you have no power. What the gambler is saying is that he can tell by looking into the narrator's eyes that he has no power. He knows that the narrator does not have a winning hand. In essence, the gambler has rendered the narrator powerless.

After the gambler tells the narrator that he is fresh out of aces, he offers to give him some advice if the narrator gives him a shot of whiskey. The narrator obliges.

The gambler advises the narrator that if he is going to play the game then he'd better learn how to play it right. He also advises the narrator that he needs to know when to hold 'em, know when to fold 'em, know when to walk away and know when to run. The gambler further advises the narrator that every gambler knows that the secret to winning is to know what to throw away and what to keep because every hand is a winner and every hand is a loser. This is advice that we all can appreciate. Some of you are in a good place. You are right where God would have you to be and in the best possible position to walk into your destiny. You have followed God's plan for your life and you can clearly see the path to your destiny from where you stand. So, in this case, you should hold on to the hand that you currently possess. Don't request another card and don't pull from the deck. Some of you are constantly pulling from the deck and still can't come up with a winning hand. This is when you have to admit to yourself that you cannot win with the hand that you are currently holding and should fold. You should lay your cards down and stop playing with that hand as you would stand a better chance at winning with the next hand. When the cards that you are holding in front of you do not measure up to God's promises for your life, then you should throw in the hand and walk away. To continue to play that hand could potentially mean that you would lose everything. Finally, after you've played the game over and over and still cannot come up with a winning hand, and the game that you are playing is _now_ playing you, then you should run because you are not equipped to play the game, and to continue to play could mean destruction.

If you are going to play the game, play to win. Always know who is on your team. It's important to know who is with you and who is not; who supports you and who doesn't. There comes a time in each of our lives when we need to take inventory of the people around us. We have to learn to get rid of folk that deplete us. We make a habit of keeping people around that don't mean us any good by making any and every excuse why we can't let them go. Some will tell you to always follow your heart, but you can't always follow your heart especially if someone is sucking the life out of you.

In the end, the narrator says that he has found his ace. What the narrator means is that he found his purpose. In the beginning, he was on a train to nowhere and now he has found his direction. He now knows where he is going. He has found the confidence that he was lacking and he now knows *who he is*. He found the peace that he'd been searching for. He found the courage he needed to make better decisions. He found his winning hand.

I encourage you to find *your* winning hand. Life is never without its challenges and risks, but if you are going to play the game, you have to learn to play the game right. Hold on to your Ace, your power, which is your faith in God. Without faith you are already declared a loser before you've had the chance to win. You have to know when to hold 'em, when to fold 'em, when to walk away and when to run. It is okay to walk away from something that isn't right or doesn't feel right because the secret to winning is knowing what to keep and what to throw away.

God has a mate for you. Our problem is that we try to make things happen in our own time. Our time is not God's time. God has a reason and a season for everything that He does. So, don't worry that you haven't met the man of your dreams. When God sends him, you will know that he is the right person because you will feel it down in your spirit. You just have to be sensitive enough in the spirit to know if the person that you are involved with is the person sent by God. If you allow the wrong person to come into your life at the appointed time set by God to bring the right man into your life, then how are you going to be in position to receive the man who God truly has for you? Will he be perfect? No, but he will be perfect for you. God will send the perfect mate for you at the perfect time. You don't have to struggle to make it happen; it will happen in God's time. All God wants you to do is stay in faith and trust that He will bring it to pass. He will bring the right person into your life at the right time.

9

NO MORE
TEST DRIVING

*No Longer
Settling for Less*

I had a conversation once with a man who told me that most men will not marry a woman unless he test drives her first. He said all vaginas are not the same and that a man needs to be sure that what he will be getting is good before he commits. I told him he was insane and that no man will ever test drive me again. My days of being a crash test dummy are over. Sadly, I've even heard Christian women say that women who are willing to sleep with men have the upper hand. I beg to differ. We have the upper hand, plain and simple, because men value women who keep their drawers up. Believe it or not, most men think that if it ain't worth working for, it ain't worth having. Do you realize the number of women men come in contact with who tell them they are celibate and with very little effort the drawers are off and running? When we tell a man that we are celibate, they expect to see the evidence. Men want to know that there are women who say they love God, are celibate, and mean it. Do you believe a man can look upon a woman and tell if she is clean? Well believe it, because it is true. I don't mean bath clean. I mean spiritually clean. A clean woman is the desire of his heart. Sure he has used women. But he used women because the women allowed themselves to be used. If the women would have only taken a stand and said 'no,' then they wouldn't feel so violated when he didn't call or come back. If we allow a man to use us for his sexual gain, then we deserve whatever we get because at any time we had the right to say no. Having sex requires two willing, *undressed* participants. Unless a man violates you and takes your body, then you are a willing participant and at any time prior to the act, you could have said no. But no... we don't want to say no. You know why? Because we feel our cat is Queen. We feel if men sleep with us, then maybe they'll want us. We think our cat is our saving grace. We think our cat will be the best he's ever had. But even the best he's ever had is still not enough to make him commit. You know what men say to that? "Damn! That was good. She got some good cat." Or, "The sex is great but I don't like her like that." When a man doesn't want us he just doesn't want us, and sleeping with him will not make him stay. We think that if we are sleeping with a man it means that we are in a relationship, but his understanding of the terms of the agreement is totally different. We should never think that because we are having sex with men that this means that we are in a relationship. Our self-esteem has gotten so low that we feel if he lies with us then he loves us. So we give it up out of desperation because it satisfies an urge that's in us all to be loved. They don't love us, they love our bodies.

When we have sex, we feel like finally somebody somewhere cares about us. No matter how long or short the act is, for that moment when he is inside us we feel loved. We feel complete. Even if we know a man doesn't want us, we still have sex with them because, it's not about whether he wants us. For that very moment, it's about fulfilling a need and that need is love. Within all of us, no matter who we are, there is a need to be loved and feel loved. Having sex with men gives us some resemblance of love. In our head we can claim it for those few seconds or however long the act takes because in our head it's just him and me even though there is no us. Although he is not feeling it, we are feeling it. For us it is different. It goes beyond the sex act and straight to the heart. A man can shake it off and wipe it off after he is done and go right into someone else. We are left with all the thoughts and he's gone past the fact that he has just ejaculated, but not us. We are reliving the moment over and over again. We relive the feeling, the whole thing; even after he has gone we are still left dreaming. And we will hold on to that until someone new comes along and gives us a new picture.

Why have nightmares when you can dream of what it's like and what it means to be with a man who truly loves you for you, is committed to you and won't walk out of your life when the sex is over?

When a man is dealing with a celibate woman he knows he has to pull out all the stops. What has worked for other women will not work for you, so he has to change his strategy. Because his desire is to conquer, he has to be methodical in his plan. He is going to prove to you that *he* is the one worthy to have you and not the other guy(s). He is aware that others have put in their application so he has to convince you that he is the better candidate. By announcing your commitment to God and your vow of celibacy, you have already positioned yourself to receive the best this man has to give. Initially his goal will be to conquer you, but as you continue to hold out, his strategy changes. His image of you transcends from that of a piece of cat to a confident and committed woman of God. The fresh scent of celibacy is driving him crazy. So, just be patient! He may not show signs of commitment initially, but, trust me, when a man knows that ain't nobody else been in your vault he will keep watch of the grounds to make sure the package is secure. He may not be able to get it, but, he is going to make sure no one else gets it either. Our resolve to keep ourselves celibate makes us more desirable. We become more desirable because men think that if we have been celibate and no one has had it in a while, then, damn, it must be good!

10

HOMEMADE IS IN

The Decision to Wait on God

I made the decision to remain celibate and wait for God to send me a mate after experiencing one heartbreak after another. One failed relationship after another. They all told me I was beautiful, gorgeous or sexy but none crossed the line to marry me. When I started on this road to celibacy I encountered many dark days and cold nights. I went through periods of loneliness. At times I didn't feel pretty. I didn't feel confident. My self-esteem was way down and I felt like there was something wrong with me. Every time I told a man that I was keeping myself for my husband they laughed. They told me that I would be single for the rest of my life. A few hung around to see just how long it would take for me to break. Others hung around because they had heard the same lame story before and they were determined to make me out to be a liar. There were times when I wondered if God would ever send that special someone. I wondered if it was possible for someone to love me enough to wait for me; someone who would marry me without the benefit of test driving me first. I was always told that a woman who keeps herself keeps her respect.

Women are not keeping themselves anymore. No one is holding cat this day and time. Everybody is having sex. Everybody is screwing, even the saved women. They say they are celibate and before you know it, they are bouncing more than a rubber ball. For some of us, all a man has to do is blow on us and the drawers go sailing through the air like a kite. Some are like dope fiends, just got to have it one last time—looking for that high that will either take them over or take them out.

Celibacy is a rare commodity. It commands respect, so what better time to be celibate than the present, a time when sexual immorality is up, sexual diseases are spreading like wildfires, divorce is at a record high, trust is at an all-time low and faithfulness is almost non-existent. This is the perfect time for us to be celibate. Celibacy demonstrates that we are able to go without. It is a discipline. It shows that we are willing to set aside our physical needs for our spiritual advancement. I know it's tough being celibate, especially when you are competing with women who are willing to have sex, but trust me when I tell you, homemade is in! Believe it or not, there are men out there who are looking for celibate women. Sure, they expect sex because women are giving it up with very little requirement, but, remember, when a man is considering a life partner, he is considering someone that he can trust. If a man lies down with $100 in his pocket he expects to wake up to $100 and not $99. He is looking for someone who will be faithful, not someone who as soon as one of his boys taps her on the shoulder the drawers come off. He wants someone who has his back, whether he has a dime or dollar. Through our celibacy he is able to see our endurance and strength. Celibacy also demonstrates our faithfulness. When a man sees that we are faithful to God and faithful to ourselves, it sends the message that we will be faithful to him.

When a man hears that a woman is celibate, it moves through his ear canal like a passenger train. It travels through his ear canal, takes a tour of his brain and crash-lands into his penis. He knows that you are not a virgin but there is something about a woman being celibate that drives men crazy. Men view celibate women as something rare, untouched, and clean. It also sends the message that you care about yourself and you care about your body. When you tell a man that you are celibate he will do one of many things.

a. He will either move on immediately because he doesn't believe you're worth the time, nor the effort.

b. He will stick around just to see how long it will take for you to give in.

c. He will respect you and your decision to remain celibate until marriage and is not just interested in making you his bed partner but his life partner.

Celibacy sets us apart from other women. It brings about a glow. It's a glow that men can see, even unsaved men. At first glance a man can tell there is something different about us and this intrigues them.

Celibacy is like a spiritual cleansing. Once the toxins have been removed from our system, our skin no longer looks dull, dark and sallow. We look clean, bright and refreshed. Celibacy is an eliminator of waste for the spiritual body as a cleansing is for the physical body. You know what your body feels like when you are eating well and exercising. You feel healthier. You feel stronger. Your body feels lighter and you feel more energetic. Well, this is what celibacy does. It washes away the sin therefore leaving behind the glow. This is why we look more youthful and feel more fresh and vibrant. Even unsaved men can see our glow.

Celibacy is more than just a word. It is a form of integrity. When you're celibate you are not out and about beyond what's normal for everyday life; you're in a reserved state in preparation for your husband. So when a man approaches you, you don't treat him badly but you are careful because your senses are keener. Celibacy polishes up all of our senses. You see everything, things you probably would have missed. You go from a place of not feeling confident to sudden inner strength. It's like you are looking through a new pair of eyes. When you listen to people, you not only hear what they are saying, you also hear what they are not saying. Through celibacy we are able to use clear judgment when getting involved with a man.

*****

I can recall during my marriage how my body would drip like a faucet just waiting on the penetration. At times I would climax just from the sheer fact that he had penetrated me. He didn't have to do anything at all. Just put it in. I used to think that he had the best penis I had ever had in my life until I realized it was all in my mind. After I made the decision to leave him, I moved out of the marital home and into my own apartment. He convinced me to come back to the marital home so that we could talk because he wanted to discuss reconciliation. After about a week apart, I went back to the marital home and we talked and made love. Making love to him was the worse experience I'd ever had. It was awful! The man that I once thought was a stud was a dud. There was no sensation. There was no pouncing. There was no climax. It was so bad that I drove back to my apartment and I cried myself to sleep. I thought how could this be? I felt like a fool, like I had been deceived, like this can't be real. At any moment I was going to awake from this nightmare and everything was going to be okay. But it wasn't. I had met and married a man who was nothing more than a deceiver. He had captivated my mind and stolen my body. And to think that all those years I couldn't get enough of him. It was all in my mind. He had captivated my mind and as a result my body felt like it was the best sex I had ever had in my life. I was seduced with words that gave the illusion of grandeur. It wasn't until God took the blinders off that I was able to see that he wasn't the great lover that I thought he was. This just goes to show you that words have great power and influence over our lives. This is why celibacy is so important. If I had kept my legs closed and gotten to know him, I would have seen him to be the deceiver that he was.

Celibacy affords us the opportunity to re-evaluate our past relationships and stand back and see a man's flaws and the hidden things that we wouldn't ordinarily see. When Jesus encountered a blind man He placed spit on the blind man's eyes and laid his hands upon him and asked him what did he see. The blind man said, "I see men as trees walking." Jesus then placed his hand upon the blind man's eyes once again and told him to look up and again asked him what did he see. At this point the man's sight had been restored and he said, "I see men as they are." When we are involved sexually we cannot see what we *need* to see. Sex blinds us. We can only see the things we *want* to see. Celibacy helps us to see the clearer picture and takes us from the place of vulnerability to a state of confidence.

11

CREDIT WORTHINESS

The Mistakes We Make When Choosing a Mate

J had to touch on this subject because every time I hear a woman say she is not interested in a man unless he has good credit, it makes me cringe. A man's worth should never be based on his ability to obtain credit.

What does credit worthiness prove?

Since when does credit worthiness determine if a man will be a great husband, one who will love you, cherish you and be faithful to you? How can credit determine if your suitor will be a good father, a great lover and your best friend? Credit worthiness doesn't determine what kind of marriage you will have or what type of provider your husband will be. Neither a man nor a woman should ever be measured by their ability to obtain credit. I know some of you will disagree with me, but before you do, let me say this:

We all have a past and in our past we have all made bad choices. We've all made choices that if life would afford us the opportunity, we would do over differently. I married a man based solely on experiencing my first climax. I thought I loved him and later made the startling discovery that I cared for him deeply but I *loved* what he did for my body. Because of my choice to marry a man for the sexual benefits, I found myself being abused every day. And, yes, he had good credit! He was the supporting spouse and I was dependent on him. When I separated from him, I had nothing. All the time I spent being in love, trying to be the perfect wife and adhering to his demands, I should have taken the time to save some money. I should have been putting something aside for my future or a "rainy day." So when I was forced to leave him, because of the abuse, I left with my kids (one growing inside of me) and $25 to my name. As a result of fighting for custody of my kids against a man whose earnings far exceeded mine and trying to keep a roof over our heads and food on the table, I was forced to file for Chapter 11 bankruptcy. Months into my Chapter 11, due to mounting legal fees, I couldn't keep up with the payments and was dismissed from the plan. I had to immediately re-file so that my car wouldn't get repossessed because my car was all I had. But because of the legal costs involved in fighting for custody of my kids, I could only maintain the payments for a short time. I was dismissed from the plan once again. This time my car was repossessed. I've been beaten, bruised, battered and broke. Should I have given up on the hope that one day God would bless me with someone who'd be a blessing to my life? Someone who will accept me as I am—someone who will not give a thought about my past? I am still the same woman—a good woman. But I am a good woman who made a horrible choice, a choice that came with great consequences. Trust me, a man is more concerned about whether I am going to have a headache every night than he is with my credit score.

We never know what a person may have gone through. There could be a whole host of reasons why your potential suitor has had credit problems or financial challenges. He could have started a business that went under and all of his personal assets were tied to the business. He could have had an illness that required hospitalization, which resulted in expensive medical bills. He, like me, could have gone through a terrible divorce. Maybe his heart led him to co-sign for a family member or close friend and they didn't meet their end of the obligation. The reasons could be numerous.

All I am trying to say is, please, don't let a man's credit worthiness decide whether he is good enough for you. A man may possess so many more attributes that will be beneficial to you, but you will not be able to see them if your radar is stuck on this one thing. Get to know the man, the whole man, before you make a decision to cancel him out, because this man could very well be the best thing that has happened to you!

The same can be said for good looks.

When we become too specific, what we don't realize is that we are tying God's hands. Instead of giving God a long list of requirements that you want in a husband, why not switch it up. Why not ask God to give you what He thinks you can handle and, more importantly, what you deserve. See, because, you've had Mr. Good Looking. Remember him? He was the one who thought he was better looking than you. He was the one who reminded you that you should feel privileged just to be seen with him and he constantly reminded you that other women were standing in line just waiting to take your place. You've had Mr. Six Figures. Remember him? He was arrogant, obnoxious, condescending, and rude. He was well educated as he had graduated from one of the top Ivy League schools in the country, but behind closed doors, when no one was looking, he was giving you black eyes and calling you a bitch and a whore. He didn't respect you, your thoughts or ideas, and to make matters worse, he enjoyed degrading and controlling you. You also had Mr. Good Body. Remember him? He was a lousy lover. He was the one who thought of himself as some Greek god and all he wanted you to do was please him. When the two of you made love, you had to do all the work. And how could you ever forget Mr. Big Penis? He was the one who came to see you with some other woman's drawers in his pocket!

Remember the time when you said you wanted a man who had a good relationship with his mom because you just knew that if he had a good relationship with his mom then he would be good to you? I know you remember him. He was the one who consulted his mother regarding every major decision in his life and only consulted with you when he needed sex.

Each of these men met the criteria of your checklist but now they have all come and gone and all you have left are the memories. Why would you want an unending stream of men coming in and out of your life, your heart and your bed when you can have complete fulfillment, true commitment and a bed of roses without the thorns?

These illustrations show you the blessings you could possibly forfeit when you tie God's hands with your checklist. All packages are not wrapped the same. Some goodies and hidden treasures will not be made known to us immediately. At first glance the package may not look exactly as you may have envisioned but I guarantee you will be swinging from the chandeliers every night. What you should do is ask God who He has for you. Ask God if who He has for you is different from the image you have in your mind. Because you've sampled the ones in your mind and they are now gone. They are gone because you obtained your credit report from the wrong credit bureau. You should have gone to the Heavenly Credit Bureau. Because the Heavenly Credit Bureau would have given you an accurate credit report. I'm not saying that it isn't good for a man to have great credit, what I *am* saying is that some won't. Those who don't have good credit with man could have excellent credit with God. Good credit with God could mean that a man refuses to cheat with other women because his wife is everything that he has ever needed. Good credit with God could mean that your husband is willing to do whatever it takes to make you happy. Good credit with God could mean your husband sending you to the moon every night and twice on Sundays without a space suit. Good credit with God could mean your husband praying and leading the family in worship. Good credit with God could mean your husband raising kids that he didn't father and treating them like they were his own. Good credit with God could mean your husband working two jobs, if necessary, to provide for his family all the while still adhering to every one of your needs. Everything that God has is good. Accept who God has for you and treat him right. If you do, I guarantee, you will skipping every day, even in the rain. While your girlfriends are dreading going home you can go home every evening to a candlelight dinner with you as the main course. And he will make sure you are satisfied before he is satisfied. Every day you will be hurrying and scurrying to get home because you know something good is there waiting for you. The best credit any of us can have is with God as this qualifies us to receive the best He has to give. Let God give you His best. Let Him give you who you need when He decides you're ready to receive it. Don't become so picky and checklist-oriented that you miss out on the wonderful treasure God has for you. Don't miss out on a chance at real love and true happiness that only God can give you in the mate he has designed especially for you. Wait on God!

12

NO WED, NO BED
The Battle Along the Way

uring the time that I began writing this book I started dating again. This gentleman and I had met the year prior to dating because our daughters were classmates. I first met him when he called to invite my daughter to his daughter's birthday party. From the moment we greeted one another at the party, we both felt something move on the inside. We only said hello during our brief interaction/encounter, but it was the unspoken words that spoke loudly. It was as if our hearts were speaking in code to one another. For months I couldn't get him off my mind. A year later he called and once again invited my daughter to his daughter's birthday party. Just as I did during my first encounter with him, I felt something this time, too. Again he didn't say much but was very cordial to my daughter and accommodating to me. A couple of days after the birthday party he sent me a text message saying he hoped we had had a good time at the party and if I didn't mind, he would be happy to come by and pick up my daughter sometimes to hang out with his daughter. I told him that would be fine as my daughter constantly talked about hanging out more with his daughter. A few months later he called to see if my daughter and I would be willing to take in a movie with him and his daughter. Fortunately for him, we had made no plans. He seemed thrilled. I have to admit, I was a little thrilled, too. I hadn't been out on a date in years. We talked for hours. He apologized for using the kids as a way to get close to me and stated that he just didn't know how to approach me. It had taken him over a year to build up his nerve to ask me out. He went on to say that he felt something the first time he saw me. He said the first time he saw me he saw a beautiful woman but he also saw something more. He had wanted to say something the year prior but he didn't feel it was the right time. He had finally decided that he was going to ask me out and he wasn't going to dance around his feelings any longer. He felt it was time for him to tell me how he felt. During our conversation, I shared with him that I had been celibate for several years and would remain celibate until marriage. He said he appreciated the "disclaimer" and he understood. He admitted that it would be pretty tough, dating a woman and not being able to make love to her, but he was willing to give it a try. He said, "If nothing comes of the relationship except a good friendship then at least I walked away with something." After hours of talking on the phone, it was official: We had made a date and were both eager to try out this new friendship. He said he felt like he had gotten a 300-pound gorilla off his back. He admitted that over the course of the year it was hard for him to focus when he thought of me. He said he noticed something different about me the first time he saw me. He said he witnessed something in me that he has never seen or felt before with any woman he has ever come in contact with.

A few months into the courtship we encountered a little turbulence. The no sex before marriage disclaimer, as he called it, had proven to be quite challenging for him. He admitted that he shared a deep connection with me and as such made it that much harder for him to resist me. He said just being around me, hearing my voice, or just thinking about me gave him a severe hard-on. He stated that he had dated women who told him they were celibate but soon after he found out they were full of shit. He always ended up having sex with them. He also told me that he had never dated a woman who he didn't have sex with. Even though we discussed my celibacy early on in the relationship, he became offended by my stance to remain celibate and mistook it to mean that I did not desire him. This angered him and he felt rejected. He felt if anyone was entitled to the cat it was him because, after all, we had professed our love to one another. He would often ask me how I could tell him I loved him but wouldn't make love to him. I would tell him if he gauged my love for him by my unwillingness to make love to him, then he would get an inaccurate reading every time. I explained to him that I was not a blow-up doll, but very much a real woman with real desires and needs. I don't know why men think that being celibate means you have no desire to have sex. They don't get it. My cat still purrs. She still acts the same as she did when she had a starring role. I think he felt that when we kissed I didn't feel anything. That couldn't be further from the truth. Truth is, when he kissed me it drove me crazy. Every kiss migrated from my lips and traveled straight down to my cat. I had to remind her that this was not an audition. When he touched me, not only did I feel the sensation in the area where he touched me, I felt it all over. There was no physical sex or oral sex because I wouldn't let him touch me below the waist and every time we saw one another I would wear snug-fitting jeans and adjust my belt tightly. This way if we ever had sex it certainly wouldn't be accidental but consensual.

Once during heavy petting and kissing, he began to massage and kiss my neck and breasts. The sensation was so overwhelming that I climaxed. I was so embarrassed. I had never climaxed from kissing and breast stimulation. I didn't even think it was possible. I also felt ashamed because the only reason I let him stroke and kiss my breasts was because I felt sorry for him. I figured this was the least I could do considering he was still hanging in there with me. But I later saw that this was wrong to do and this actually made matters worse. The more I gave the more he wanted. He was no longer satisfied with just a piece of me, he wanted it all. The more I spoon-fed him the angrier he got. He felt a sense of entitlement. He felt as though he had put in time and work and was deserving of my body. He began to hit me where it hurt—in the heart. He started staying away and curtailing the calls. He started distancing himself from me. He began to distance himself more and more but I still wouldn't give in. Then he went completely silent on me. No phone calls and no text messages. His strategy was to weaken me to get me to the place where I'd feel like I just had to have him or die. To make me bow down to his demands. To make me concede defeat. I knew it was nothing more than a game, a trick to get me to give in. It was tough and very hurtful but I stuck to my guns.

He wanted sexual commitment and I wanted commitment sex. He wanted me to commit to having sex with him and I wanted him to commit before sex. I desired him sexually just as much as he desired me. The only difference was the route we'd taken to get there. I found myself constantly telling him how much I loved him and that I desired him, too, but all this seemed to do was frustrate him even more because that's not what he wanted to hear. What he wanted to hear was he could have it! He figured that in time I was going to change my mind and time had come and gone and I still hadn't changed my mind. He felt because he has been with celibate women in the past and was able to make them crack that the same tricks would work for me. He figured me to be a nut like the rest. He knew I was a nut that would be a little harder to crack but a nut nonetheless. He told himself that the more time he spent with this nut (me) that he would eventually crack it. What he didn't realize was that I was no ordinary nut. It takes a special nutcracker to crack this nut.

✸✸✸✸✸

As women, we have to stand our ground and realize that we are valuable. We have to have sense enough to know who we are and that our bodies shouldn't have to be inspected and tampered with to assure a man that the goods are *good*. We are God's "good thing" and that should be enough for us. But because we are sensitive by nature, we feel like we have to give him a little something to hold on to or a little something to hold him over because, after all, he is still in the game and you haven't given him any yet. It is sort of like our peace offering. We feel like because they put pressure on us to sleep with them that we have to do it to make them want us. We feel the need to leave the door slightly ajar because he could just be the "one." We have to be careful when we leave the door open—we set ourselves up to be robbed because some men are like thieves. If a thief sees any opening he will come in. Once he's in, he will take everything of value that he can carry. When a man starts removing our possessions we don't even notice they're gone. We didn't see him take anything. It's not until we are left standing empty that we realize we have been robbed. All the while they were stealing right from under our nose, but we were too caught up to see it. We let them steal from us because we love them and we care. They were able to take everything we had because we didn't arm our alarm system. They stole our hope. When that wasn't enough, they came back and stole our dreams. When that wasn't enough they came back and stole our confidence. When that, too, wasn't enough they came back to steal our heart.

The thief came to take anything that was of value and because you left the door open he re-entered until he finished the job. He has taken everything you own. He stole your hope only to find there was nothing to steal as he soon discovered the hope chest was empty. He came back to steal your dreams only to find that your dreams were worthless because they were never going to come true. He comes back again, this time to steal your confidence only to leave empty-handed because your confidence was stolen by the prior thief. He returns because he knows there must be something of value that you possess. So he comes back one final time to steal your heart because it's the only thing you have that could potentially profit him. Once he has your heart he knows he's got you. He doesn't want commitment. He just wants to take what he can get and leave.

It's like a man walking into a cafeteria. He enters the line and selects his meal choices only to find that there is no cashier at the end of the line. So what does he do? He eats, he drinks, he takes his napkin and wipes his mouth and he leaves nice and full and it was all for free. He didn't have to pay a dime. A man feels as though there is a field of female cows and he can milk every last one of them for free. So he tells the farmer that he doesn't need to pay him for his milk anymore because he is getting it all for free. What does this do to the farmer's business? It causes his business to suffer. That which was once valuable (his cows) providing an income for him and his family is no longer profitable. Its worth has been decreased because it's now free and free holds no value. You don't have to win any special contest to get what is free. Free is available to anyone who's motivated enough to go and get it. It's on a first come, first serve basis until the product runs out. We should no longer feel obligated to give ourselves to men for free. Even escorts get paid for their service and here we are giving it away for free. No wed, no bed!

13

THE WEIGHT
Waiting for God's Best

Once during my many trials of celibacy I dated a guy who I thought was the "one." He knew I was celibate and at first didn't seem to mind. Months later as we were discussing marriage, he told me that he wanted to marry me, but, first, he wanted to make love to me. He gave me this guilt trip about wining and dining me, etc., and the sacrifices he had made in the relationship. He said that after all he had done for me the least I could do was take care of his needs. After weeks of hearing him nag, I gave in. I gave him the cat. How stupid of me. Did I give in because he required it or did I give in because I wanted it? Obviously, I wanted him to make love to me or else I wouldn't have given in. After we did it, he didn't marry me. In fact, it wasn't long after I gave it to him that he broke up with me. I felt used and abused. I felt like trash. A couple of years later, after he was done playing with a few stray cats, he called and asked me to marry him. I told him, "no." I asked him why he didn't marry me when I wanted to marry him. He said he didn't have a reason to marry me because I had already given him what he wanted. I thought, how arrogant. He didn't marry me because he had gotten what he wanted. What does this mean? This means that after I had sex with him I lost my leverage. He got what he wanted and soon after reduced me to used goods. No longer of use to him, I was discarded like used tires. The game was over and he had won. I was rendered powerless. I had given my power to him. I had lost my ability to negotiate.

When we meet a man and tell him that we are celibate and turn around and have sex with him, we lose our leverage, our ability to bargain. We reduce our chances for commitment because he has now gotten what he wants. Also, their perception of us changes. He now has a very different image of who we are. If marriage is what you desire, then you should not have sex with a man because it is easier to get him to commit when you don't have sex with him. The longer you keep yourself the better your chances are for commitment. Once they have had sex with us there is no need for commitment because they've gotten what they wanted. Another thing, keeping ourselves makes us more attractive to men. It pleases a man to know that no other man is checking in and out of us like a hotel.

I asked a few men that I know if they could marry a woman without having sex with her first. They all said, "yes" they could but only if the woman possessed other desirable and interesting qualities. None were specific as to what these qualities were. One said that he could do it if he felt a connection with the woman and felt like she had much more to offer than just sex. It's important that you understand that when men see us, they see "sex." The first thing they see is someone to have sex with. Their No. 1 goal is to conquer. Trust me, when a man meets you, he does not have falling in love on his mind. For him, love comes later. We love sooner and men love later. You are seeking a life partner and he is seeking a sex partner. That doesn't mean that it will always be this way but it is important to know that it will remain this way until the relationship balances out. Before you decide to sleep with a man, give him a chance to see who you are. Give him a chance to see that you are a special and unique woman, unlike any woman he has ever encountered. Let him see your best qualities and how they can be an asset to his life. Be different. Show off your best self. This is your time to shine so shine brightly. But don't try too hard. Just relax and be yourself. Spend much of the time talking to him, find out what makes him tick. What gets him going. What makes him happy. What pisses him off. What are his likes and dislikes. Some things you won't have to ask him. All you have to do is be observant. Listen to what he *is* saying and hear what he is *not* saying.

Waiting is never easy and for some it can be very difficult. While we are waiting we go through periods of uncertainty. This is the hardest part of the wait and it is called the weight.

The "wait" is the time period from when God says He is going to do something to when it comes to pass.

The "weight" is the period of uncertainly between the promise and fulfillment of the promise; the emotional toll that we sometimes face while we are waiting. While waiting you may experience one failed relationship after another. You may even wonder if you'll ever love again. You wonder if you'll ever trust again. You think back on your previous relationships and you feel betrayed. You thought that person would be the keeper of your heart, to hold it, cherish it, and protect it, but instead they bruised it and tossed it aside. Now you feel ashamed because you once trusted that person and believed he loved you and that this was the relationship that you would be in for the rest of your life. You were looking for a life partner and in him you believed that's what you had found. With him you felt like you were atop Mt. Everest and now you feel like you are at the bottom of the sea. Your self-image has gone from one hundred to zero. Your whole emotional state is off. You don't feel pretty anymore. Even when someone tells you you are pretty, you don't believe them. You say to yourself that they're just lying. They're just trying to make me feel good. They're just feeling sorry for me. There may be times when you feel like life isn't worth living. So, you cry yourself to sleep every night or awake to emotional bouts of crying. You blame yourself. This spins you into a state of depression. You wonder what you did wrong. You ask yourself what, if anything, you could have done differently. You tell yourself that you messed up and ask yourself what you could have done differently to change the outcome. You tell yourself that if you had done this right and that right, then maybe he would have stayed. You begin to tell yourself that if you were prettier he would have stayed or if you hadn't gained weight he would still find you attractive. You second-guess everything. You become a recluse. You don't talk to friends and family members, especially the ones who are happy in their relationships. The last thing you want to hear about is how happy they are. You feel like a vagabond just wandering around. At such a time, encountering a homeless woman you say to yourself, "I know exactly how she feels because I, too, have lost everything." You think the only thing that separates you from her is that you have a place to call home. You feel helpless and hopeless. Your faith has diminished and you begin to doubt if God hears you at all. You begin to wonder if God, too, has cast you aside and you think no one understands what you're going through.

The Transition

Then God sends someone to reach out to you; to extend a hand to you, to pull you out of the dark closet and lead you into the light to show you that you can live. Probably someone you don't know. A perfect stranger. Someone who has worn the same clothes as you. Someone who can tell you she knows where you have been because she has been there, too. Someone who tells you there is hope and that God has someone very special whom He has created just for you. Someone who tells you that God has never forgotten about you.

Right when there is no hope, Hope shows up. God will send a word at our lowest point. Sometimes through a perfect stranger, through our dreams, through the pulpit, and/or through a movie. A word from God just for you that will change your life. A word that will encourage you, nurture you, strengthen you and inspire you.

For some, we will meet our husbands in our worst-looking state. When he sees you, he doesn't see the unkempt hair, the baggy sweatpants, the big t-shirt or the run-over sneakers. He looks beyond the dark sunglasses that cover your eyes, as you were trying to disguise the dark circles and bags so no one will know you have been up all night crying. He has to bend down just to look at your face because your head is hanging low. He tells you you are beautiful, but you don't believe him because you know what you saw the last time you looked in the mirror. He asks your name and you turn to walk away but he won't let you escape. You wonder, what does he want with me. The more you try to shake him the more persistent he becomes. He won't take "no" for an answer. After much persuasion you finally agree to go out with him and your life changes. You go home and reflect on the encounter as you prepare for your date. You take off the baggy sweatpants, the big t-shirt, the run-over sneakers and the dark sunglasses, since you had dressed according to how you felt. You comb your hair and put on makeup. The next time he sees you, he tells you that you are the most beautiful woman he has ever seen. He is speechless but not surprised as he recognized your beauty the first time he saw you. He knew it was there all along. And your first date is for the rest of your life.

14

THE WAIT
Receiving God's Best

After making the decision to become celibate, my intention was to remain celibate until marriage. Well, let's just say I fell of the bicycle a number of times before I managed to keep the handlebars straight. After bruising my knees, I've finally met celibacy with success.

Waiting to have sex is not easy. I know because I am waiting, too. Waiting is especially tough in the early stages of celibacy because you think every man you meet is the "one." At least that's what your vagina wants to believe. Every part of you will go in a different direction and you have to try to figure out how to pull it all together. You will eventually learn to build up a tolerance in your mind, but your body will need a little more conditioning.

In order for you to have success with celibacy, you need a strong spiritual foundation. A strong spiritual foundation is the glue that brings the major players (the heart, the mind and the body) together so that they are on one accord. This was the mistake that I made in my earlier attempts at celibacy and why those attempts were short-lived. I didn't have a strong spiritual foundation, a personal relationship with God. This is important because when you find yourself in tempting situations your pastor may not be available to give you instructions or pray with you. It is important to build a personal relationship with God because He can be where others can't and at a moment's notice.

✳ ✳ ✳ ✳ ✳

Years after Maurice and I broke up, we continued to maintain a friendship. At times he would come to visit and try to persuade me to have sex with him. Just seeing him would make me cry. I don't mean cry from my eyes. I mean cry from my cat. The mere sight of him would make my cat cry, literally, so much so that my undergarments would be soaked. He didn't have to touch me. My body was ready to surrender. And, boy, didn't he know it! Once, as soon as I opened the door to him, he grabbed me and pinned me against the back of the door. As he did so, he started kissing me passionately and ripped my pants off. After ripping my pants off, he picked me up and carried me to the sofa. He grabbed my legs and pulled them apart. He then began to perform oral sex on me. The moment his mouth made contact with my vagina everything went black. My body melted and my legs puddled around his shoulders. Everything happened so fast. During the ordeal my body wanted him to make love to me but my mind and my spirit struggled with the idea. My body wanted desperately for him to make love to me. My mind wanted a commitment and my heart, well, she was caught in the crossfire because I still loved him.

Through the years, he and I had had several conversations about sex and I had repeatedly told him that I would not sleep with him again unless we were married. He would often remind me that I said I was celibate before, but I still slept with him.

As I tussled with him to break free, he clamped his arms around my legs restraining my movement. I felt like I was in a battle for my life. I almost counted myself out because I felt that there was nothing I could do. I began to panic because I just knew it was over. He was about to make a liar out of me. Then instantly God spoke to me and told me to break free in my mind. Of course I didn't know what this meant. Then God told me to stay alert and don't consider the moment because if you do, he will win and he *will* penetrate you. My body was having the time of her life but my mind was not a willing participant. I asked, "God what do you mean?" He told me once again to break free in my mind. Now here I am with this man's head between my legs. I'm trying to listen to what God is instructing me to do and trying to stay alert and not become overwhelmed with passion. There was no doubt that he was going to penetrate me. I had to act quickly because things were going downhill fast. I could still hear God telling me to break free in my mind. Finally, after much coaching, I decided to use my mind.

Our mind is the power source which controls how our bodies respond. I used my mind to command that the power supply to my vagina be cut off. I literally instructed my vagina to shut down. I knew I had to shut down my vagina long enough for me to get my head together so that I could make an intelligent decision. I had to take control of the situation or else he would be the one with the control. When my mind sent the message to my vagina to shut down, my vagina said "message received" and she shut down. I couldn't feel anything. It was as if all sensation to my vagina was cut off. I could no longer feel his tongue thrashing my vagina. I knew he was still between my legs because I could see him but I could no longer feel the sensation. This is the benefit of a strong spiritual foundation. I would not have known what to do if God had not instructed me. I was ready to throw in the towel. I was prepared to give the victory over to the enemy. I had declared him the victorious one. But thanks to God for His Word which tells us that He will never leave nor forsake us even in the midst of temptation.

After the oral sex, he undid his pants and attempted to penetrate me. As I lay there with my bottom half exposed, he was standing over me with his penis in hand. I was frightened because the door to my vagina was open to him and all he had to do was walk in.

As he tried to penetrate me, I grabbed his penis and looked up at him and told him flat out—no! I told him I was not going to have sex with him unless we were married and I meant it. He saw that I was serious and he let me go. Boy, was I messed up afterward. My mind had won the battle but my body bucked like a wild ass for about a week.

※ ※ ※ ※ ※

Always remember that your mind is your power source. Your mind is much more powerful than your vagina. Your mind transmits messages to every part of your body. When you make up your mind that you are going to remain celibate until marriage, no doubt your body will throw a tantrum. She will be mad as hell because you have placed her on a meat-restricted diet. It will take her some time, but she will eventually get used to it. Every time I made up my mind to remain celibate, sex was running through my mind every day all day long. It seemed as though I spent more time thinking about sex during celibacy than when I was having sex. Thoughts of sex were driving me crazy, until I learned to conquer those thoughts. Now, after being celibate for some time, it doesn't drive me anymore. I realize that I am the driver. I am the one with the control. Sex doesn't control me. I control sex. I control when I will and won't have sex and with whom.

Even though I've been celibate for years I am still very much a woman and I am still attracted to men. I love men. I love the way they make me feel when our bodies collide. I love the way they contort my body to their pleasing during sex. I love the way they arch their backs and the strong masculine silhouette of their shoulders cascading over me when we make love. I love how their love muscle throbs and rises for the occasion; how it stiffens and grows with stimulation. I love all of these things about men but I know there is so much more to men than what I've seen and/or experienced. I decided I wanted more than just hot and steamy, and wet and wild. I want to experience real love, true commitment, and uncensored and uninhibited passion.

I love sex. Sex is a beautiful and fulfilling interaction between a man and a woman, but there is no emptier feeling than when a man has sex with you, zips up and leaves. What I've had has been good, but what I want is—great! I want more and I want better. In fact, I deserve better and I want the very best that God has to give. I want someone who will love me for who I am. I don't want some sort of fictitious love that seemingly appears to be intact just so long as a man's dick is inside of me and mysteriously disappears when he zips up. I want to experience the kind of love that bursts forth the moment the two of us look upon each other's face; one that only the two of us can feel. I want a love that loves me for who I am. I want a love that will carry me through all the seasons of life and even as I grow older makes me feel like a little girl again. I desire a love that surpasses all the fairy tales I have ever read and all the loves stories that I have ever seen. I imagine experiencing passion that penetrates so deeply that it penetrates my soul and reaches depths that no man has ever reached before. A passion that makes me shed tears because I've never experienced such ecstasy.

I envision my husband taking his time to make love to me so I can savor every moment. I also imagine him looking up at me every now and again during foreplay because he wants to make sure that everything he is doing is bringing a smile to my face. I think what a thrill it must be to experience passion so deep that during lovemaking I completely lose my mind because I've never had it in that fashion. Passion that is so heated that even when I'm trying to play it cool and hold back, the moment he touches me, my body betrays me. Even more powerful than that, I imagine passion that is so raw that God tells the angels, "Come on let's give them some privacy."

This is what waiting means to me. Celibacy is not about going without sex. Celibacy is about waiting to have the best sex of your life. So, is it worth it for me to go without temporarily so that I can enjoy a lifetime of fulfillment? Yes! Is it worth it to me to say "no" right now to say "yes" to my husband later? Absolutely! So, please, don't view celibacy from the standpoint of not having sex. View celibacy from the standpoint of having the best sex of your life. This is the kind of love that is worth waiting for.

Before I go, I would like to encourage you to keep a positive outlook on life. Think positive thoughts, speak positive words, and engage positive people so your life can produce positive results. Even when there is a high probability of impossibility, be positively persuaded that your worst days are behind you, better days are ahead of you, and the best is soon to come.

God bless you.

ADDITIONAL READINGS

All the
Single Ladies

ver been in a relationship that left you in the **red?** You meet a guy. The two of you begin to date. You conclude that he is the one. You begin to invest time and resources into building a relationship. Then you arrive at a place where your rent or mortgage is behind, your car note is past due, your lights are turned off, you have no money to buy food, you have no money to put gas in your car, your bank account is overdrawn, you can't provide for your children and you find yourself borrowing money to pay this bill and that bill. When you get paid you still don't have enough to cover the past due bills, the current bills or pay back any of the money that you've borrowed.

Has this ever happened to you or someone you know? Why is it that we find ourselves in the red or overdrawn when certain people come into our lives? I'll tell you why. It's all in the math. Relationships are like bank accounts. If you continue to withdraw money from a bank account without depositing money into the bank account, then pretty soon you'll find yourself in the red. If you're in a relationship and you continue to put out and the other person is not putting anything back into the relationship, you'll find yourself in the red—*overdrawn*. The relationship has drained your resources because you have not required the person to make a contribution. You decided that in order to be in the relationship you had to give to prove your love, and all the time that you were giving he was taking. At first it doesn't seem like a big deal because you figure you can afford it, but after a while it catches up to you because, as I stated, it's all in the math. If you continue to put out and not require your partner to put in, you will eventually overextend yourself and come to nothing. In the red not only implies financial depletion. In the red also signifies that you have arrived at a place where your life is stagnated—things are no longer progressing. At one time a highway of blessings led right to your door and now it seems the highway that the blessings once traveled is blocked.

So, how do we find ourselves in situations like this—overdrawn? There are many reasons, but let's just start with two. The two main reasons why women find themselves in relationships with men who add no value to their lives are—(1) fear and (2) lack of confidence. Fear that no one else will come along and not confident enough to believe that they deserve better. Quite frankly, some women believe more in running over than running out. Translation—having a piece of man is better than having no man at all!

I've heard this phrase a million times and I'm sure you have, too, but what does this really mean? What is a piece of man? A piece of man is a man who only gives a <u>piece</u> of himself, and that little piece is more than enough for you because it is all that you require. What can you possibly do with a piece of man? Relationships are supposed to add value to our lives. How much value can a *piece of man* possibly add to your life? Please don't misunderstand me. This does not mean that you should not seek to build a relationship with a man who earns less than you or a man who earns little. What I am saying is that you should want to build a relationship with someone who is willing to take what he has earned (substantial or small) and put it back into the relationship for the advancement of the relationship. Having a piece of man means that you are in a relationship with a man who is only adding a *piece* of whatever it is that you need. You should not want to be in a relationship with a man who is only willing to give a piece of himself; you want a man who is all in, a man who is willing to sacrifice all that he has for the furtherance of the relationship.

We also find ourselves overdrawn or in the red because we have no patience. I cannot begin to tell you how many times I've heard of women moving men into their homes. What happened to the time when men made these provisions for women? What happened to the time when women *required* that men make these provisions? If the man is too slow in making a commitment or the necessary provisions to further the relationship, we become impatient and step in by suggesting that the man come live with us. But what are we really suggesting when we propose that a man come live with us? Actually, we are not suggesting anything. What we are doing is forcing commitment. Oftentimes when women ask men to come live with them it is because they are fearful that he will not commit. Having a man live with you provides a sense of security, though false, that he is yours and he is committed to you. This forced commitment does not guarantee true commitment. There is no commitment in a house key. The commitment is in the heart of the man, and if it is not in his heart to commit, then he won't.

Finally, another reason why we find ourselves in the red is because we have no faith or little faith. God wants you to have healthy and loving relationships, but in order for you to receive the blessing you must trust God and have the faith to believe that He will not mismanage your life. Trust Him for your mate and be confident in His choice for you. It may seem like He is moving a little slowly, but your delays are part of God's plan. God loves you and wants nothing but the best for you, but just because God loves you does not mean that you cannot end up in a bad place. You have to make the right decisions and be cautious of who you let come into your life. God's will for your life is perfect and He knows what you need, and when something is perfect you cannot improve upon it. Be confident in who you are. When you are confident in who you are, you will not accept any person just to call him your man.

Last Word

This was a hard message to write. Some of you will appreciate this message and some of you will stone me for writing it, especially those of you who see yourself in the message. However, this message had to written because as I talk with women, it appears that women are still willing to sacrifice everything even though they are receiving nothing or very little in return. It is unfathomable that women are willing to accept demeaning and degrading conditions just so they don't have to be alone. Women are sacrificing their finances, their bodies, their homes, their careers and, in some cases, their children for the sake of relationships. If you are in a relationship and you are doing all of the giving, this might be a great time for you to re-evaluate your relationship because chances are he is not the one for you. If you always have to invite a man out on a date and pay for his companionship, then he is not that into you and you don't mean as much to him as he claims. Some of you will find truth in this message and some of you will carry on in the belief that having a piece of man is better than having no man at all and for this reason will always find yourselves in the red.

All the Single Ladies
PART II: RECALCULATE

ver wonder how a man can be in a relationship with a woman for years and never marry her and meet someone else and marry her in a matter of months? In order to appreciate this message you must read the previous message, "All The Single Ladies," because again, it's all in the math. Relationships are like bank accounts. If you continue to withdraw money from a bank account without depositing money into the bank account, sooner or later you will find yourself in the red. If you're in a relationship and you continue to put out and the other person is not putting anything back into the relationship, you will eventually overextend yourself.

Every morning during my commute to the office I listen to the Strawberry Letter on the Steve Harvey Morning Show. If you are a listener of the show, then you are familiar with the Strawberry Letter and are aware that the majority of the letters are written by women with relationship issues. Many of the women express that they are in "on again/off again" relationships with men. To hear a woman say that she is in an on again/off again relationship always seem to irritate Steve as he exclaims that there is no such thing as an on again/off again relationship. He insists that a man is NEVER off! He further exclaims that if a man is not ON with you then he is ON with someone else.

So, how can a man be in a relationship with a woman for years and never marry her and meet and marry someone else in a matter of months? Most men know exactly what they want in a mate and for this reason likely will not settle. A man will stay with a woman for years all the while contemplating his next move. Unlike us, a man will not stay in an unfulfilled relationship and accept that this is the best that he can do. When a man believes that he deserves better he sets his sights on better and will stop at nothing until he gets exactly what he wants, even if it takes years. If a man believes that it is obtainable he will go after it—whether it is a career goal, a sports car or a woman. Women on the other hand seem to settle more often because of the two reasons mentioned in the previous message—fear and lack of confidence; fear that no one else will come along and not confident enough to believe that they deserve better.

Additionally, men don't like to be alone. A man will use you as a "filler" until he finds the woman he really wants to be with. A filler is a woman who provides services to a man, such as sex, money, meals and companionship. The woman usually has no idea that she is just a filler and that her services are only temporary as she is led to believe that she is in a relationship. A man will spend years with her because she is providing him with these essentials. The filler is also led to believe that the promises he's made have contributed significantly to the relationship. It is not until she writes a check that bounces that she realizes that her account is overdrawn. Why doesn't she realize sooner that her account is overdrawn? She doesn't realize it because she has been recording promises as credits in her check register. He made her promises and every time he made her a promise she recorded the promise in her check register as a credit to indicate that the promise was good. At a glance it appears that they have made equal deposits into the relationship because the account shows a surplus. But upon closer inspection and recalculation, she discovers that her deposit entries were *actual deposits* and his deposit entries were all *broken promises*. She now realizes that she was the only one making deposits into the relationship.

A wise woman once told me that relationships are not as hard as people think. She said the problem is that many of us are too busy watching the commercials when we should be watching the movie! This means that many of us are paying more attention to the things that don't matter and less attention to the things that do. We hear what the man is saying but we're not listening to what he's not saying. I speak to you from experience as I was once married and on the day that I left my ex-husband I only had $25 in my checking account. It was all the money I had to begin my new life. I struggled for years because I invested in a relationship that did not invest in me. I was too busy laughing at the commercials and not paying attention to the movie that was playing before my eyes. It wasn't until the movie went off that I discovered that I was in the red. I wondered—how could this be? How could it be that I am left with just $25 after investing so much? After sitting down and balancing my checkbook it appeared that my check register was full of promises. I had recorded promises that he made as credit entries in my check register. It took me years to recover and now I can watch as many movies as I please because I invested in someone who invested in me. I invested in God and God invested in me. Now I can sit and laugh at the commercials without fear that I will be left in the red when the movie is over.

If your relationship has left you in the **red,** here is what you need to do. You need to recalculate! You have to handle your relationship like you handle your finances. If someone asks to borrow money from you, your philosophy should always be... ***don't loan anything that you cannot afford to give away and don't give away anything that you cannot afford to lose because chances are you might not get it back.*** You must learn how to properly balance your checkbook. You cannot record promises as credit entries in your check register because, if you do, your account will show a surplus when there is no surplus. Finally, you should never invest in someone who is not willing to invest in you. If a man is interested in building a relationship with you, he will take that which you have deposited and reinvest it back into the relationship to build a reserve so that the relationship can prosper.

Last Word

Ask yourself... If a man is not making deposits into your relationship then where is he making his deposits?

Recalculate!! Balance your checkbook! I am not telling you that you shouldn't follow your heart. But you must keep in mind that the heart's job is to feel. The heart is not capable of reasoning. If you decide to follow your heart, please be sure to take your head along so that you are able to discern what is right and true. Always remember that promises hold no value unless they are made good, so never record promises as credit entries in your check register or else you'll find yourself with a checkbook full of broken promises and a pocketbook full of broken dreams.

Choosing the Appropriate Level of Coverage

When choosing a health insurance company, how do you determine which company will provide the best coverage for you and your family? When choosing a partner, what criteria do you use in determining if the person you have selected will provide the best level of coverage for you and your family?

Every year, our employers host an open enrollment where we select medical, dental and vision insurance providers for the upcoming benefit year. The open enrollment process can be grueling as there are many different insurance companies to choose from. Some companies offer several different levels of coverage. You would choose one of these plans based on your family's medical needs. If you are fairly healthy, you would probably choose basic or low-level coverage. If you have a few medical concerns, you would probably choose a higher level of coverage.

Choosing an insurance company takes careful planning. Most of us select our health insurance companies based on the following criteria: the best coverage, at an affordable rate, that will meet the current and long-term medical needs of our family. We take great care in choosing the appropriate level of coverage, so why not use the same criteria when choosing a partner?

We should choose a partner like we would choose our health insurance company—*very carefully!* We should always seek to choose someone who will provide the best coverage at a rate that we can afford. After all, what is the purpose of insurance? The purpose of (medical) insurance is to cover the costs associated with health-related expenses, i.e. routine physical exams and check-ups, lab tests, prescription drugs and various other expenses that you would otherwise have to pay out of pocket if you were not covered. Other insurances like auto, home, rental, personal property, etc. help us to manage the risks associated with loss, theft, fire and injury. We never know when we will need it, but we pay our premiums because it gives us peace of mind that we are protected in the event of such occurrences and it minimizes our financial responsibility.

For this reason, you should choose your partner like you would choose your health insurance company. You want someone who will provide the best coverage for the best price, someone who will meet your current and long-term needs. You want someone who will provide financial support, who is mentally suitable and spiritually compatible, who shares your interests and adds value to your life. A person who believes in you, shares your dreams and aspirations; who is supportive, but provides you with the space to flourish. You want to choose a person who supports not only you, but also loves and supports your children as well.

It is important that you choose a person who enhances your life because when you fail to attract the kind of relationship that enhances your life, your dreams will drift farther and farther away. Things that should have taken you one year to accomplish will take you five years or better because you didn't have the right person in your life to foster progress. Instead, slowly and quietly, the relationship is bringing you down, and if you are not careful, you will one day look in your rear view mirror and see your dreams traveling down the road.

When God wants to bless us He sends us somebody. When the enemy wants to set us back he sends us somebody, too. My pastor once said that relationships are like elevators. They will take you up or take you down and sometimes the movement is so subtle that you don't even realize you're being taken down until you reach the ground level, and, trust me, this is a premium that you cannot afford! So, don't put yourself in a situation where you are not adequately covered. If you do, you are setting yourself up for failure and heartache. Also, remember you are NEVER in a relationship alone. Relationships affect everyone around you. If you have children, when you hurt they hurt, when you cry they cry and when your heart aches their heart aches, too. This is *why* it is important to choose a partner who will provide an adequate level of coverage for you and your family. Our happiness is our responsibility and it has everything to do with the people with whom we build relationships. When paying a premium into a relationship, you should have peace of mind in knowing that you have selected someone who will be good to you and your children and foster progress in your life. Relationships should increase our value and take us to the next level. So, choose carefully and choose wisely. Choose your partner like you would choose your health insurance coverage, so that you may have the appropriate level of coverage for you and your family.

Last Word

Choose your partner like you would choose your health insurance company—the best coverage at an affordable rate that will meet your current and long-terms needs; a relationship that is loving and supportive where you will not have to sacrifice your resources, your family or your dreams and passions that will meet your needs currently and for years to come.

About the Author

Barbara Dempson is the founder of She-Attitudes™ - a multimedia, publishing and entertainment company. She is the Creator and Executive Producer of **"It Don't Hurt Now"** - a theatrical production that deals with helping to heal women who have suffered abusive relationships.

Barbara founded She-Attitudes™ to promote her inspirational work **"The She-Attitudes"** (© **2001**). The She-Attitudes© is ten affirmations that inspire, empower and uplift. Barbara calls The She-Attitudes© her personal love letter from God. The She-Attitudes© were given to her during a tumultuous period in her life – a period when she found herself being physically abused, feeling hopeless and helpless. Barbara built her company around these inspirational messages to offer hope, restore faith, transform lives, and to help women discover their purpose.

The success of her production, *It Don't Hurt Now*, led Barbara to expand She-Attitudes™ to a multimedia and entertainment company to provide a platform for others to transform their life journeys into books and multimedia productions.

Barbara Dempson was born and raised in Durham, North Carolina and currently resides in the Washington, DC area.

To learn more about Barbara visit her website.
www.barbaradempson.com